THE COMIC CON
DEE LAGASSE

You are a superhero!

All Lagasse

For every woman who has been told or made to feel like you couldn't do something just because "you're a girl."
You are enough. You're more than enough. You're a superhero.

there is honesty in the lies—
　　the art we spill from
　　mouths, & hands,
　　& hearts—to this world
　　& to each other.

there is beauty in these
　　mirrored worlds—
　　where we tell each other
　　things we need,
　　things we *should know,*
　　honest confessions for us alone.

there is life in this bending—
　　compromising where we can,
　　steady mouths,
　　& hands,
　　& hearts, where we cannot.

there is honesty in this love—
　　not looking for permission,
　　not asking for the applause
　　when fiction & reality blur.

we can do this every day, *all day*:

the world spinning faster as we touch,
the world fading as we close pages,
& chapters, & doors,
existing for us— *this us we have written*—alone.

J.R. ROGUE

BiRDiE 1.

I HAVE NOTHING TO WEAR.

It's only the single most important day of my life, and I have absolutely *nothing* to wear.

My bedroom floor, which is currently covered in unsuitable clothing, would argue otherwise. Luckily for me, bedroom floors can't talk.

Of course, like the proper procrastinator that I am, I find myself in this dilemma with just an hour to spare before needing to be out the door.

"Caaampbeeell!" I yell, throwing myself back onto my bed.

"...always something. What's the mat—" A concerned voice mumbles down the hall, growing louder as my best friend of over twenty years approaches. When her words stop short of being complete, I know she's made it into my pit of despair. "Um, Birdie. You *are* aware your closet exploded, right?"

"I can't go. I have nothing to wear."

"Oh, stop being dramatic."

I can imagine she's simultaneously rolling her eyes and

shaking her head right now. The tug on my leg that drags me halfway down the bed is unexpected.

"What the hell, Campbell!" I screech, grasping onto the fitted sheet underneath me as if it'll give me traction.

Spoiler alert: it doesn't.

When I sit up, I'm flooded with contradicting emotions. On one hand, there's complete admiration. On the other, there's jealous hostility.

Cascading jet-black curls fall just below her shoulders. The bold plum tones of her eyeshadow give her silver-hued blue eyes a vibrant pop. And beyond her magazine-worthy hair and makeup, she's found the *perfect* outfit: a fitted white scoop neck T-shirt tucked into a navy swing skirt that's covered in white polka dots. A tan belt and matching ballet flats tie the outfit together, giving her the business casual *boss babe* look I would kill for right about now.

Okay, kill *for* is a bit of an exaggeration. Murder isn't exactly in my wheelhouse, but ugh. This bitch. If I didn't love her so damn much, I would hate her.

"Get up," Campbell demands, narrowing her eyes. "You have clothes. Lots of clothes. You're going."

"Fine," I concede. "But I need help. What the hell am I supposed to wear? It's not like I can show up in yoga pants and a graphic tee."

Ninety percent of my wardrobe consists of just that—*yoga pants and graphic tees*. Oh, and black leggings.

There isn't a dress code for working from home. When I do have to attend events, I usually just wear black leggings and—you guessed it—a cute graphic tee. Chances of there being a super-hero on it are greater than not.

"I *told* you we should have gone shopping," she reminds me as she steps into my almost empty closet. "Wait! What if I told you that you could still wear a graphic tee?"

"I'm listening." I chuckle, looking down at my watch to check the time. "But you better tell me fast because we need to leave in fifty-five minutes."

As she talks about pairing a *Suffra-Jette* graphic tee with the lone navy blazer still hanging in my closet, I nod, half listening. The all-consuming nerves that sent me down the *I need to have the perfect outfit or my life is over* spiral return the moment she says the name of my comic.

My comic.

The success of *Suffra-Jette* was a surprise to everyone, but especially me. Named after the suffragettes of the women's movement in the early nineteen-hundreds, it was only supposed to be a four-part miniseries for National Women's Month a few years ago.

It was the first female-led original comic printed by Coolidge Comics & Collectables, a comic shop turned hybrid small press publisher and storefront in Maine. Within days of release, the print edition sold out in comic shops across the country. The digital e-book hit the top ten on Amazon. We debuted on the USA Today *and* Wall Street Journal bestseller lists—something almost unheard of for comics, but especially for a small press.

Since then, we've sold more than a million copies across the world. The first issue secured the spot for the third most comics sold—coming in just after *Star Wars* #1 and *X-Men* #1. We made history. A women-led comic written by a team of women, outselling the likes of *Fantastic Four*, *Batman*, and my childhood favorite, *Spider-Man*? Unimaginable.

Don't get me wrong, the numbers are an incredible feat, but no amount of sales can compare to knowing what we've given to our readers. Letters from girls as young as five and women as old as ninety flooded the store from all over the world. I made the time to respond to every single one of them and have kept them all. Every piece of fan art I'm tagged in on social media gives me just as much joy as the first one did. It never gets old to be asked to sign a comic book or to take a photo with someone at a convention.

A million little things had to line up perfectly for this kind of success. I could never pinpoint the exact variable that made it happen, but my Jette was an instant hit, and she shows no signs of slowing down anytime soon. Less than a year after its first publication, *Suffra-Jette* got its first offer from Hollywood. And then its second, and then a third. Within a month's time, there were a dozen offers, from small indie film companies to the big production company *Suffra-Jette* ended up with.

I spent months working with little to no sleep, drinking my weight in energy drinks to keep up with creating the storyline for new issues while helping write the script for the movie. It's rare for creators to be given such a significant role in the development of a movie. I did what I had to so I had the time to be on set—starting with today's table read.

But, before anything else, I need to get out of these damn pajamas.

And I should do something with my hair.

ATTICUS 2.

WHEN I WAS A LITTLE BOY, I wanted to be a superhero. But not just *any* superhero. Though I loved them all, Spider-Man was always my favorite.

I had Spider-Man bedsheets, toys, comics—you name it. After three Halloweens of getting the same Spider-Man costume just one size bigger, my aunt tried to convince me to be *anything* else. So, I went as Peter Parker, Spider-Man's secret identity. I was nothing if not consistent.

Now, at twenty-eight, I would like to think I've grown beyond being the little boy that lost his mind over a silly-string web shooter watch, but the knot in my stomach as I approach the conference room implies that I have not.

The opportunity to be in a big-budget superhero film seemed unattainable when I first started in this industry at seventeen. It was as big as dreams got. Something so far-fetched that saying it aloud seemed silly. I'm not superstitious by nature, but I was terrified that if I spoke it, if I brought life to the idea, I would jinx it somehow.

Granted, I'm not exactly playing Spider-Man. If anything, I'm the Mary Jane to Peter Parker's Spider-Man—and I almost turned the job down because of it. Call it pride or whatever you want, but I had this idea in my head of what I wanted, and this certainly wasn't it.

One afternoon with my sister and aunt changed that. All it took was Eliza putting on *Wonder Woman* and Aunt Bea gushing about how Chris Pine embodied the perfect feminist supportive role to Gal Gadot's Wonder Woman to know I needed to take the audition.

The audition was merely a formality. Haley Powell, *Suffra-Jette's* director, called my agent and told her that if I wanted the job, it was mine. Come to find out, the *Suffra-Jette* comic team had asked for *me* specifically. Another thing I never would have imagined.

After a decade of being in the industry, I would consider myself a seasoned actor. But from the eight-season teen drama that gave me my start to the Oscar-winning World War II biopic that sent me traveling the world for over a year of my life, I've only taken roles that would be the best move for my career. The smart move. The safe move. I've never taken a job solely because I wanted to. Until *Suffra-Jette*.

All it took was a once-over of the script for me to know I needed to be in this movie in one capacity or another. And I told the casting director exactly that after my screen test. I didn't care if I was Guy #4 From the Coffee Shop. I just wanted to be a part of the magic. Which starts today with the cast table read.

Most of us have read the script a time or two by now, but this will be the first time we'll read it together. It will also potentially be the last time we're all together until the premiere.

Filming isn't what people might expect. There's no perfect formula. Shoots can last for five minutes if you get the perfect take, or it can take hours—days—to get the perfect scene. There are early mornings and late nights. Sometimes both. You can go a week and a half without being on the call sheet, and then suddenly you're on there for three weeks straight. You can shoot the ending first, the beginning in the middle, and the middle at the end. No movie is the same. More accurately, no director is the same.

I've heard nothing but wonderful things about Haley. She's collaborated with a few friends of mine, and they've all said the same—working with Haley Powell is unlike working with any other director. As a former child actor, she understands just how grueling filming can be. Unless it's necessary, she shuts down production every Saturday and Sunday to give the cast and crew a break. Everyone is invited to grab food from meal services at any time. Actors on her sets are allowed to voice their opinion and improvise if the scene allows for it. Whatever it takes to make everyone comfortable and create the best version of the film *together*.

All of that paired with an incredible script made me decide to take the role. However, Eliza and Aunt Bea will *absolutely* take all the credit if you ask them. And that is why I'm eager to meet Haley for the first time. I want to thank her for including me in this project. I also want to thank the women of the *Suffra-Jette* comic book team. I don't know what I did to deserve their attention, but they changed my life with their request for me in the film.

There's a group of women gathered at the head of the table with scripts in hand. I guess I'm not the only one that was taught that early is on time, on time is late, and late is unacceptable.

Looking around quietly, I'm surprised to see that Haley isn't here—and that I only recognize four of the women in the group. Of those four, I've met three of them.

Violet Lee, Ms. Jette herself, is in the midst of the group. Her outfit makes me smile—a black fitted tank top with the neon *Suffra-Jette* lightning bolt symbol and a pair of jeans that have a flare so big they could put any disco dancer from the seventies to shame. Her hair is a lot shorter than the last time I saw her, cut into a sleek bob—much like the one the character she will portray wears.

Zoe Adams is *Suffra-Jette*'s penciller, and the one with the bright candy-apple red hair. She and her husband own the comic shops and the publishing house that exclusively distribute the *Suffra-Jette* comics.

The day after I was officially cast as Otto, my agent reached out to let me know the Adams wanted to take me to dinner. I had no idea what to expect, but three hours and about a thousand dollars in sushi and sake later, they both felt like old friends. In fact, I've golfed and gone to a few Red Sox games with Isaac Adams and Bishop Vaughn—the president of Coolidge Comics—a handful of times since then.

Campbell Porter, *Suffra-Jette*'s social media director, stands with her phone in hand, ready to take a photo at any given second. We went "live" together on *Suffra-Jette's* Instagram last week, and she sent me the sweetest email afterward thanking me for my time. I'm already a fan of hers based on that alone.

And then the curvy brunette with an ass like a peach? That's Birdie Yamamoto.

She's the creator and lead series writer for the *Suffra-Jette* comic. Birdie and I haven't spoken a word to each other. As soon as I landed the role, I looked her up on social media. I had every intention of shooting her a message, asking her if we could meet for lunch. After reading the script—that she helped write—I really wanted to do justice to her character. I still do.

But when I say I chickened out the second I scrolled through her feed, I might as well have been sitting there with my phone in hand going "cluck, cluck, cluckity, motherfucking cluck." I don't often find myself intimidated by people—big roles, criticism, and my own self-doubt tend to be the source of my anxiety. However, I would be lying through my bleached white teeth if I said that most of my nerves today weren't from coming face-to-face with Birdie.

From afar, I admire her talent immensely. I bought every issue of *Suffra-Jette* and devoured two other series she had worked on before. Somehow, she's managed to create an original space for her characters while bringing important topics to the forefront. Her art is incredible.

With Google at my fingertips, it was easy to find her and discover a little bit about her before the movie's preproduction began. The first thing I realized when doing my "research" was that Birdie Yamamoto is quite possibly the coolest person on the planet.

Vocal in her stance on women's rights and equality, she uses her platform to highlight social injustices. She often shares photos of her family, vegetarian dinners, and sketches of flowers —though she'll be the first to shut down any idea of her being an artist if someone tries to tell her she should draw for the comic book. Come to think of it, I don't think there's a single solo selfie-style photo on her entire feed. Every photo she's in, Birdie is with someone else, and it's clearly taken by another person.

I try my best to hang back undetected. People have been known to change their demeanor in my presence. They assume that because I've acted in a few important things, I've lost sight of the fact that I'm a regular guy who gets up every morning, gets dressed, walks his dog, and goes to work—like everyone else. My work just isn't the traditional nine-to-five.

I haven't, though. That's why, if it's only for a few moments, I want to catch a glimpse of who these women really are. Almost immediately, Violet notices me lurking. Expecting my cover to be blown, I brace myself to put on my best *fake it till you make it* smile.

Instead, I have to hold back a chuckle when I hear her ask them what their thoughts are on me being cast as Otto—Jette's love interest.

Men aren't known for blushing, but I can feel the warmth settling in on my cheeks when Zoe lets out a little laugh and redirects the question to Birdie.

"How about you take this one, B?"

From Zoe's side profile, I can see the grin growing wider on her cheeks.

"Yeah, B," Violet eggs her on, stealing a glimpse at me from the corner of her eyes. "Tell us your thoughts on Atticus."

"Way to throw a girl right under the bus, Zo," Birdie says. The thick braid of hair sways back and forth as she shakes her head. "Um, well... uh... let's just say Campbell and I started watching *Sunset Heights* because he was shirtless in the show preview, and I kept watching it for seven years after because he continued to take his shirt off."

I could have let it go on, but who am I to waste an excellent opportunity handed to me on a silver platter?

"So what you're saying is there's a good chance you'll sign these comics if I take my shirt off?"

BIRDIE 3.

MORTIFIED DOESN'T COME CLOSE.

Betrayed comes to mind, though.

Violet owes me nothing. We met ten minutes ago. And in Campbell, Ramona, Margot, and Francie's defenses, they all had their backs turned like me. But Zoe? That little traitor knew I was walking right into a setup. Not only did she not throw up smoke signals, flash lights of warning, or I don't know, stop me from humiliating myself in front of a *world-famous* actor, she fucking shrugged the moment she saw the sheer panic on my face.

Traitor, I tell you.

I may or may not be overdramatically reacting to the situation. But Atticus Cohen just heard me admit that I've had a crush on him for about a decade.

Holy shit. Okay. Breathe, Birdie, breathe.

I'd like *things I never would have said had I known he was standing right behind me* for a thousand, please.

Since there's no sand for me to bury my head under in this conference room, I—far from willingly—accept my fate and turn to face the man who will be bringing Otto Jackson to life on the big screen.

In the two point seven seconds I have, I try to think of something clever to say. *Anything* that would allow me to recover from my fangirl moment.

And nothing comes to mind. Me! The girl who has an opinion about everything. I always have something to say. *Not this time.*

However, even if I could figure out how to bullshit my way out of this, any plan of action would have been forgotten about the second I turn and see the way the light catches his ice-blue eyes.

I wonder if it's too late to make amendments to the script. The role Atticus is playing is a regular person with no superhuman powers. I'm thinking his character needs revised. He could be from an alien planet, or a god of some sort. We need to think of something. There's no way to explain a human being this attractive.

Perfect example: Marvel chose Chris Hemsworth to play Thor.

He might have also been the best actor for the job, but he was the best-*looking* actor to play the god of thunder. I read somewhere that Tom Hiddleston auditioned to play Thor too and, don't get me wrong, I love him as Loki, but I couldn't imagine if they had cast him as Thor. Or even Liam, Chris's brother, who also auditioned.

No. Marvel got it right when they cast Chris Hemsworth.

Just like we got it right by choosing Atticus. But if I could just tweak the script a teensy bit...

Obviously, I knew long before today that Atticus is good-looking. Hell, *I'm* the one that asked Haley and Nova if there was any way we could get him in for an audition. As for Jette, no matter how hard I tried, I couldn't envision her in my head. The casting director nailed it with Violet.

Otto has always been Atticus, though.

When I described his physical appearance to Zoe so she could draw him, I said, "Atticus Cohen. He's Atticus Cohen."

And she really brought him to life. Otto has perfect little dimples, broad shoulders, and tousled sandy-brown hair that falls into place perfectly. Just like Atticus.

But seeing him in photos or behind a television screen and then in person is comparable to seeing in high definition for the very first time. It's beyond anything I could have expected.

I laugh nervously when I realize everyone is still looking at me, waiting for my response to his question. "You can keep your shirt on." My voice and hands both shake as I reach out to take the small stack of comic books from his hand. "I'll sign them just because you showed up with them."

Violet waits patiently for me to take the comics before pulling Atticus into a warm hug.

"Atticus, may I introduce the incredibly talented *Suffra-Jette* team?" She steps back, pointing to each of us one by one. "You know Campbell and Zoe. Birdie is the cutie patootie holding a stack of your comics. And here we have Ramona Spencer, Francie Evans, and Margot Raymond."

"Just missing Nova Vaughn, right?" Atticus calls out our editor by her full name as his eyes dart between us with uncertainty.

"Yasss!" Francie nods in approval. "We stan a man that does his homework."

The moment is surreal to say the least. Of all the cast, Atticus was the last person I expected to show up with a first edition printing of the comic and to know Nova—by name nonetheless—was the only one missing from our team.

Turning to Campbell and Zoe, I show them the first comic on the stack—a special variant cover of the first issue. "There were only five thousand of these printed."

"So that would be why I had a hell of a time finding it." Atticus chuckles. "You don't want to know how much I paid for it."

"I mean, *I* kind of do." Francie shrugs.

Francine "Francie" Evans is the boldest person I know. If Zoe and Violet hadn't pulled their little stunt when Atticus walked into the room, it wouldn't have surprised me to see Francie walk right up to him and introduce herself.

With her half-shaved head to her platinum blonde hair, she's always making a statement. Even her attire today—a black crop top with "Feminist as Fuck" written across her chest and hot pink leggings—was no doubt chosen to draw attention. She's the queen of one-night stands, fake names and numbers, and bright red lipstick.

But even Francie's face softens when Atticus tells us he paid close to two thousand dollars for our little comic that originally sold for three dollars in the store.

He doesn't elaborate and there's no chance to ask more questions before three more cast members join us in the room. A mix of excitement and jitters settles in my stomach when Haley and Nova Vaughn walk into the room together.

"Good morning, everyone," Haley calls out, silencing the room. "Why don't we all take a seat? Let's get everyone's drink orders as people start coming in so we can get started."

Nova leans in and discreetly points over to where we're standing. Haley's eyes lock with mine as they make their way over to us.

I can't help but think there are much more important people than me in this room, but Nova, Haley, and I co-wrote the script for the movie together, and that experience bonded us forever.

It could be said that Nova is singlehandedly responsible for my career. She took me under her wing when I was just a lowly unpaid intern at Cobalt Comics—the company we both started at. When she left to work for Zoe and Isaac at Coolidge Comics & Collectables, she brought me with her. I wouldn't be here today if she hadn't let me tag along.

When the contract was signed for film rights, Nova and Zoe made sure their husbands negotiated our comic team having an active role in the entire process. Most comic book writers never get to be as involved as I have been. There have been stories of comic books turned into blockbuster movies and the creators get a mere thank-you card and a check for a few thousand dollars. Writers have gone to world premiere parties, only to find out they're not on the list.

"Wait. So does that mean Atticus won't be taking his shirt off?" Francie asks lowly as we each pull out the black leather office chairs in front of us. "What a bummer, huh?"

My jaw clenches and my shoulders stiffen in place. I get it. We all had a nice little laugh at my expense, but it's time to move on. I open my mouth to tell her just that, but clamp it back shut when Atticus steps beside me.

"Is this seat taken?" Atticus asks, motioning to the empty leather chair in front of him.

There are name cards in front of every seat in the room. He's placed in the middle of me and Violet because the three of us will be reading the most today.

"It is now," I say as he settles into his assigned seat.

"So I hear you're a New Hampshire girl," Atticus begins once I've sat down too. "Us New Englanders should stick together. Rumor has it…" Narrowing his eyes down at the table, he leans in and lowers his voice. "Ryder is a Yankees fan."

I don't really follow sports, but you don't grow up in this region—specifically with a dad who loves the Red Sox—and not know about the rivalry between New York and Boston.

However, Ryder Donegan, who is playing Otto's dad *and* the villain of our little story, is Hollywood royalty. I'm not sure when he arrived, probably when I was making a fool out of myself in front of Atticus, but I'm glad I missed it. Not that it really matters *when* he got here. Now that I know he's here, my nerves have grown tenfold.

He's just a human. He breathes the same air as the rest of us. He's here because I wrote this story.

Nope. Not helping the nerves. Not even a little. In fact, I'm sure I just made it worse.

Once everyone is settled in their seats, assistants begin making their way around the table, taking drink orders. Since Campbell and I hit up the hotel gift shop for caffeine as soon as we got here, I just ask for a bottle of water.

"Water for me too, please," Atticus tells her when she inches in front of him. "And a black coffee, two sugars."

"I think I can handle that, Mr. Cohen," she purrs, batting her eyelashes at him. "Anything you need, *anything at all*, I can get it for you."

Normally, I'd roll my eyes at her blatant flirting, but honestly, I don't judge her for shooting her shot.

What does surprise me is the discomfort the attention gives Atticus. He shifts in his chair as he nods curtly. "Thanks. I'll be fine with just the water and coffee, though."

Assistant girl doesn't skip a beat, or take a hint, reaching over to place her hand on his arm. "Well, if you change your mind—"

From the other side of Atticus, Violet clears her throat. "I would like an iced lavender latte and a bottle of distilled water."

Violet raises her eyebrows, apparently unimpressed by Assistant Girl's advances. Assistant Girl continues to move down the line after jotting down Violet's order, never looking back to Atticus. Once everyone's drink order is in, Nova stands up from her chair.

"Hey, hi, hello!" she says, her voice timid and quiet. This is the first time I've seen her nervous. As an editor, Nova is tough. There is no such thing as a deadline extension. She picks apart storylines and is known for the extensive rewrites she often requires from not just me but her other writers too.

As much as *Suffra-Jette* is my baby, it's also hers. It was the first project she was named editor on. We created this world together during so many late nights that turned into early mornings. She ripped up the first draft and shredded the second. Anything less than perfect wasn't acceptable.

"First, thank you all for being on time." Nova beams, looking around the room until her eyes stop and linger on Francie and Ramona.

The corners of my lips curl as she subtly calls out their perpetual tardiness and then introduces the *genius*—her word, not mine—behind the comics, *aka me.*

Giving the room a small wave, I flip open to the first page of the script. When Zoe told us the production team invited us to the table read, she also tasked me with reading the scene descriptions in the script, likening it to being a narrator in a play.

I accepted, not thinking I had much of a choice otherwise. I imagined this moment only about fifteen thousand times since she told me I would be taking an active role today. I had dreams about stumbling over my words, opening my mouth and nothing coming out, my voice shaking... But as I begin reading, my shoulders relax. I know these characters. They are mine.

"Scene opens with Jette, a woman in her midtwenties, fastening a utility belt around her waist. The sound of her alarm clock beeping catches her attention. She takes a sip from her coffee mug as she walks over and turns the alarm off. The clock reads five..."

ATTICUS 4.

"SITTING ATOP AN ELECTRIC POLE, Jette looks over the city. At the sound of sirens, there's a visible electric charge from her body. Fade to black while the bridge to 'Midnight Sky' by Miley Cyrus opens the closing credits."

Every eye in the room is on Birdie as she lets out a breath and places the script down on the table. I'm not sure who starts clapping first, but it doesn't take long for everyone else to follow suit. If I weren't the one that was lucky enough to get the seat next to her, I would miss the quiet "Holy shit" that leaves her lips.

Zoe, making no effort to hide the tears streaming down her cheeks, reaches across the table to hand a box of tissues to Birdie, mouthing, "I'm so fucking proud of you" midpass. Then, as if planned, Campbell scans the room with her phone just as Francie starts and successfully gets the entire room to chant Birdie's name.

What you *can't* plan is the admiration every woman on the *Suffra-Jette* team has in their eyes for the woman sitting next to me. It's enough to make water pool in my own.

"Can I hug you?" I ask Birdie amid the applause. "I feel like this a huggable moment."

Pulling her shaking bottom lip in, she nods. At that, I push myself back from the table and stand. As soon as she's upright on her own two feet, I wrap her in my arms. While we're in such proximity of each other, it's impossible not to notice the light floral fragrance of her perfume. It's subtle. Just enough to draw me in and make me want to stay in our embrace a little longer than what one might deem professional.

"All of this is because of you," I say before letting her go. "Your story brought us all together. *You. Did. This.*"

After we break our hug, she wipes the tears from her eyes with one hand and gently pushes me with the other one. "See what you did? It's not necessary to be that damn charming, Atticus Cohen."

Crooking my head, I squint a little, pretending to be puzzled by the nature of her statement. "Isn't it, though?"

She doesn't get the chance to respond before Haley makes her way over to us.

"I don't think I've ever been so excited for a project!" Haley squeals as she approaches us. "Campbell needs to borrow you for a few minutes, Atticus. Something about scheduling interviews and lives. You know me and social media."

I chuckle. "Ha. You and me both, Hales. You and me both."

My stance on social media is well known. For the longest time, I was only on one platform. During interviews, when people ask the cliché question: "What would you tell your younger self?" I always answer with, "Stay off social media."

It has a multitude of benefits, I get that. Being able to connect with people all over the world at any given second is an incredible tool. But I've also seen firsthand how detrimental it can be. Keyboard warriors think they're untouchable and that their words don't affect real people. Typically, the fellas make comments about my acting. Which is fine. I know most of them are sitting at home on their couches.

It's the women that are the cruelest. And most of the time, whatever they have to say isn't even about me. I've had "fans" who have made my exes cry because of the horrific things that have been said about their appearance. Awful, heartless things that—I would hope—no one would ever feel okay saying to someone's face.

Scanning the room, I find Campbell chatting with Nova and Zoe. Before I head out, I need to talk to Campbell about the press schedule, so I make my way over to them.

"Atticus, perfect," Campbell says. "I wanted to discuss a few dates with you. I know there isn't much to talk about yet, and you will be in over your head with press junkets right before release, but I wanted to schedule some time preproduction to record a few segments for social media. I also wanted to talk to you about an interview with Jason Franco of Pow! Press."

Oh boy. This is about to get really weird, really fast.

"Yeah. Um... listen, I don't want to be that guy," I start, "especially not right away. I'm more than willing to do anything for the *Suffra-Jette* team, but I will not be doing any interviews with Jason Franco."

"Jason's a dick, but Pow! Press is one of the biggest platforms for comics. Alienating him is a bad move, Atticus." When Nova sighs in frustration, I know I have no choice but to explain myself.

"That's why I met with him after he called my agent for an interview following my 'live' with Campbell last week," I begin hesitantly. I have spent every bit of my career practicing professional courtesy, even when people didn't deserve it. There isn't an article or interview out there that has me badmouthing a single person in this industry. "He came to the interview with an angle that I was purposely offered more money than Violet. His primary goal was to give me no choice but to make a public stance of my disapproval. I managed to combat everything he threw at me this time, but he was hell-bent that *Suffra-Jette* is a feminist publicity stunt, and I only made a big deal out of the salary difference because it would look good in the headlines."

Which couldn't be further from the truth. As soon as it was leaked that Violet would be making five hundred thousand dollars—compared to the three *million* dollars I was making, plus up to an additional two million in deferred compensation based on box office sales—I skipped all levels of professionality and went right to the production company myself. At first, they tried to argue with me, claim that contracts had already been signed, there was nothing anyone could do, blah, blah, blah. So, I offered to make up the difference from mine. And with that came three more male members of the cast offering part of their salaries as well. Between the four of us, we got her close to five million dollars base salary and up to another four million based on box office sales. Rightfully so, making her the highest-paid actor on the call sheet.

I didn't say a damn thing to anyone other than Violet and my agent. I didn't do it for credit. I did it because it was the right thing to do. It was Violet who made the statement telling everyone that I "spearheaded a campaign to make sure she got paid not just equally but more than her male castmates."

I knew there would be some media attention from it. What I didn't expect was the likes of Jason Franco to twist it into an ignorant and incredibly sexist stance. I'd never walked out of an interview until that day. I want this movie to succeed. More than that, I want the women of this movie to succeed, and in order to do that, I cannot give Jason Franco a second more of my time.

Zoe's brows furrow in confusion as she looks around me. Then she excuses herself and hastily jogs to the boardroom exit.

Just as she's about to leave, she stops short and turns back to face the room.

"Oh, and Atticus?" she calls out, locking eyes with me. "Don't worry about that interview. Isaac and I will handle Jason Franco."

BIRDIE 5.

ONCE EVERYONE HAS GOTTEN up from the table, I pop the cap off the permanent marker Atticus brought with him and begin swirling my signature on the cover of each comic. When I get to the first *Suffra-Jette* issue, I sigh happily.

Atticus is already proving I made the right decision when I suggested him for the role of Jette's boyfriend, Otto.

Otto's character isn't driven by ego or power like so many other male arcs in the superhero world. He is strictly Jette's boyfriend. He's supportive. He worries while the love of his life is out there fighting the big battles, but he stands by and lets her take care of shit.

Everyone loves Atticus because he's "hot." He has tight abdominal muscles, a strong, perfect jawline, and a devastatingly handsome smile, but it's more than that. It's the side of him that doesn't get blasted across the tabloids that made me want him for the role.

He's the guy that trekked three miles in the pouring rain for a fundraiser walk for his local animal shelter—the same shelter he adopted his dog from. He sponsors lunch for the entire school district of his hometown every year. Recently, he was in the news because he made sure Violet was the top-paid cast member of the movie, taking a decent-sized cut from his own check to ensure so.

And today... he shows up with my comics. Not just *Suffra-Jette* either. There are issues of other series I've worked on mixed in here too.

With every signed issue in hand, I scan the room and find him chatting with Zoe and Campbell.

Perfect.

I can totally ask Campbell to get a picture of the two of us for the *Suffra-Jette* social media.

Would it be pushing it if I asked him to hold up one of my comics?

I mean, that's why we're all here—according to Atticus, anyway.

Not wanting to be rude, I hang back while he finishes telling Campbell, Zoe, and Nova, "that *Suffra-Jette* is a feminist publicity stunt."

I'd never quite understood what it means when someone says something feels like a punch to the gut until this very moment. My stomach twists in agony as the taste of hot bile rises in my throat. Anger bubbles like lava under my skin when I hear "made a big deal out of the salary difference because it would look good in the headlines."

To make matters worse, Nova, Zoe, and Campbell just fucking stand there, silent with wide eyes as he spews such vile hatred from his mouth.

I should have walked out of the room with every single one of those comic books. It takes all my willpower to quietly place them on the table and leave the room without saying a fucking word to anyone.

I cannot cry here. I cannot cry here. I. Can. Not. Cry. Here.

The tears brimming in my eyes are a byproduct of my anger,

not sadness, but fuck if I'll let Atticus or anyone else see that he got to me.

"Birdie!"

Just as the elevator doors open, Zoe calls out from down the hall. Since it's just me in here, I press the close door button before anyone else can join me—or Zoe can get close enough to see me.

A tinge of guilt gnaws at me in the form of another knot tightening in my stomach. Zoe is one of the greatest people I know. She certainly doesn't deserve for me to be acting like I don't hear her, but I need to get out of here.

Out of that room, out of this building, out of the state.

If I don't put some space between Atticus and myself, I'm going to cause a scene.

As soon as I'm behind the safety of the closed doors, I pull out my phone and tell her I was just feeling overwhelmed and wanted to get out of there before the attention shifted to me and my emotions. Then I ask her to give Campbell a ride home since we came together.

I assume she'll call me out on my bullshit. We both heard everything Atticus said, but instead, all I get is:

Campbell: *Aw, babe! Of course. Please drive safe! LOVE YOU.*

Despite the fact that my stomach knot has grown into a full-blown excruciating twist, I keep myself from coming undone until I'm secured within the safety of my car.

There's no pain as my fists fly against the steering wheel. As soon as I make impact, though, the severity of the moment pulls me under like a tidal wave. Searing frustration and embarrassment continue to course through my veins, the unsettling notion that Atticus fucking Cohen made a complete fool of me—in front of my friends and co-workers nonetheless—causes my heart to slam into my chest. Fast, steady tears fall freely down my cheeks.

The salty warm taste from my tears lingers on my lips as I grasp the steering wheel with my still-shaky hands. The need to hold onto something to regain control is all-consuming.

I should have known. There had to be a catch somewhere. Everything was perfect. Too easy. From the initial launch of the comic right up until I walked over to give Atticus his comic books back, everything had fallen right into place. Then that asshole had to go and ruin everything, and there isn't a damn thing I can do about it.

This entire project is a massive deal to everyone at Coolidge Comics. Not just for the *Suffra-Jette* team but also for Isaac and Zoe as business owners. Nova and I both have our names on the line as script writers. We're setting the precedent for small publishing houses.

And it isn't just our team. Haley was given a massive budget from the studio, and they expect her to deliver accordingly.

I'm going to have to play nice with Atticus.

I'm going to have to pretend like it didn't feel like he took a knife to my heart when he sat there and so easily belittled everything that I had worked so fucking hard for. At least in his presence.

There's only one place on this earth that can bring me out of this foul mood, so I grab my phone and call one of the two phone numbers I know by heart.

"Hi, pumpkin. How'd it go today?"

The voice that greets me on the other end of the phone instantly puts me at ease.

"Hey, Dad. Are you home?"

BIRDIE 6.

EVERY SECOND of the forty-eight-minute drive from Boston to my childhood home was spent dramatically—and poorly, I might add—singing at the top of my lungs. I've had a better grasp on a few breakups than I do on this situation with Atticus.

It isn't entirely because of Atticus, either.

Sure, the things he said were awful, and I have no choice but to hate him now, but it isn't all about him. This is about me. This is about all the time and energy I put into Jette. How long and hard I worked on making sure this movie script was perfect. I was so proud of myself, and hearing him say those things put some serious doubt in my head.

What if no one takes us seriously? What if we flop? What if everyone hates it? Atticus and Violet are phenomenal actors, but what if my story isn't strong enough? Does everyone think the way Atticus does?

On the other hand, fuck him.

Fuck Atticus Cohen.

If we weren't good enough, we wouldn't have been offered a

multimillion-dollar movie deal. Our little *feminist movement* was good enough for him to sign on to and pull in a Hollywood elite like Ryder Donegan, Jr.

I wish I could settle on one emotion. All this back and forth is giving me nauseating whiplash. It's as if everything I could feel was tossed into a blender on high this morning. The highs and lows are extreme on one end and then the other. But I'm determined not to let Atticus get the better of me again.

We did this. *I* did this.

Fuck Atticus Cohen.

And if he doesn't believe in *Suffra-Jette*, that's his problem. Not mine.

You know what? How about one more time, just for good measure...

Fuck Atticus Cohen.

And besides, any additional comfort I may need to get through this is just a few feet away. The yellow ranch-style house itself isn't anything special. In fact, every house on the street looks the same on the outside. I mean, sure, they aren't *exactly* the same.

The vinyl siding and shutters vary in color from house to house, but the structure is the same—three bedrooms, one and a half bathrooms, an eat-in kitchen—even down to the placement of the windows on each house. It's cookie cutter, but I am grateful for this home. This whole perfectly matched neighborhood. Because much like my parents did, it embraced me.

I wouldn't have anything if it weren't for them—if it weren't for my mom. Who knows where I would be if it hadn't been Annie Yamamoto that found me outside of the fire station that cold December morning.

There was no note, no blanket. It was the middle of winter and they just fucking left me there. The security camera footage in the nineties wasn't the best, and whoever it was, was smart enough to wear a hood and keep their head down, so they weren't caught on camera anyway.

While her husband was deployed overseas with the Marine Corps, Annie stayed behind in his hometown, working as a receptionist at the fire station her brother-in-law captained.

Knowing proper procedure, she took me to the police station immediately. But as soon as an officer told her I would go to a state facility, she just couldn't bring herself to leave me there. It's like those stories of a wife bringing home a puppy when her husband is at work. Except, you know, my dad was a Marine halfway across the world, and Mom brought home a newborn.

They were just twenty-three. Newlyweds. But as my dad tells it, no one was surprised when they found out Annie refused to leave me. She was the girl that volunteered at the local animal shelter three days a week. Their two dogs were rescues. And every year on her birthday—since she was eight and found out that one of the little girls in her second-grade class was homeless and didn't have food—she hosted a food drive. She still does. Her heart is as big as the sun, and she loves with all she has.

Because of everything Mom did so selflessly for everyone else, the community of Townsend banded together to make sure I had everything I needed. Long before the days of online crowdfunding, hundreds of people came together, and piece by piece, they built an entire nursery and a full wardrobe for the first year of my life.

My parents still have the VHS tape recording of the six o'clock news that covered our story. There are dozens of newspaper clippings saved in a box in their closet that featured stories about my mom finding me, the first time my dad met me, and the day I officially became a Yamamoto through adoption.

No one came forward to claim me. Six months after Annie had brought me home, a judge terminated any rights my biological parents had based on child abandonment. Another six months after that, I legally became the child of Kenji and Annalise Yamamoto. Almost a year to the day after I was left on the steps of the fire station, I was given a name, an identity of my own—Birdie Grace Yamamoto.

To this day, I have no history of or any idea where my biological family is. As soon as AncestryDNA tests became available, my parents offered the option to me. Even at fifteen, I knew I didn't need a vile of saliva to tell me who my family is.

My *mom* is the one that got no sleep for the first year of my life. She's the one that went to every doctor's appointment. My *dad* is the one that worked sixty hours a week as a prison guard after retiring from the Marine Corps so I would want for nothing in my life. I was afforded a life that few children—never mind children left on a fire station step in the middle of December—get to live. I knew it as a child. I appreciate it as an adult. Which is why there is nowhere else I would rather be right now.

"Hello?" I call into the house as I slide my flats off and place them on the shoe mat next to the door. Mom's SUV wasn't in her spot, but Dad's truck was in the driveway.

"In the kitchen, pumpkin."

As soon as I step over the threshold into the kitchen, my dad turns from where he's standing, mixing something in a bowl. His ear-to-ear smile drops, and his forehead pinches with worry at the sight of me. In hindsight, I should have checked my face before I came inside. I'm not a parent, but I imagine there's nothing quite like having your daughter stroll into your kitchen at four o'clock in the afternoon with black-mascara-stained cheeks and bloodshot, puffy eyes.

"Who do I have to kill?" he asks, wiping his hands on a dish towel.

"Where's Mom?" I rebut his question with my own.

My dad has always been slightly overprotective. He's never been the "If you don't bring her home by ten, you'll meet my shotgun" kind of dad. More like the *silently judging you for not holding a door or walking on the side closest to the road* kind of dad. The kind that expects you to make the choice to do the right things for the right reasons at the right times. The "you better be willing to move heaven and earth for my daughter or you're not good enough for her" kind of dad.

"She went to the store to get your wine." You would think at almost thirty my palette would have refined a bit, but nope. Give me that cheap Franzia Sunset Blush, and I'm happier than a pig in shit. "And some celebratory cake. Now answer my question."

I have every intention of telling him that it's nothing and leaving it at that, but as soon as he side-eyes me, I tell him everything. By the time I'm done, Mom has joined us in the kitchen, and in true Annie fashion, she tries to see the best in him.

"Maybe you misheard him," Mom offers, which earns her a hard eye roll from both me and Dad.

"Or maybe he's just a dick," Dad counters. "Well, at least you can be on set without being starstruck now. I can imagine it might be hard not to get swept up in all this. It's very cool stuff. But now that you know Atticus is a jerk, you won't be intimidated by being around him."

My mom's eyebrows arch higher and higher as my dad continues to talk.

"Can we just move on?" I ask.

My phone ringing in my purse gives me a momentary reprieve.

I sigh when I see that it's Campbell. She'll keep calling unless I answer. And if I don't answer, she'll show up. The only downfall of having your childhood best friend and roommate as one of your co-workers is that there really is no safe place to hide. Ever.

"Hey, Cam," I answer.

"Don't you 'Hey, Cam' me like you didn't run out of the conference room like a bull was chasing you," she says. "Are you okay? What's going on?"

"I don't know." A pang of guilt settles in my stomach when the lie leaves my lips. "I was fine and then I wasn't. It's like suddenly—"

"It became real. Yeah. I get that," she offers. "However, on that note, I had a second reason for calling. I wanted to check in on you but also give you a heads-up that you're going to have a guest at the signing tomorrow."

Well, shit.

ATTICUS 7.

CAMPBELL WARNED me that the signing would be a big deal.

I didn't realize *how* big of a deal until I pull up to Coolidge Comics & Collectables and see the line waiting outside the door and down the street—two hours before the event is set to begin.

And this is all for *Suffra-Jette*. No one knows I'm coming tonight.

Zoe and Isaac decided to make my appearance a surprise when Birdie vocalized her concern for the event. I don't know if Birdie intentionally replied all to the email Zoe had sent out last night, but she made it clear she was not a fan of the idea.

While I can certainly understand the appeal of having Mr. Cohen attend the signing, I would prefer we keep it concealed until the event itself. Suffra-Jette fans look forward to this night every month, and I would hate for it to become the Atticus Cohen show—taking the focus off the new issue.

My first instinct was to immediately go on the defense, but after staring at my email for a good ten minutes, I realized she was right. It would be a welcome surprise for all the established fans, but if people knew about me being there ahead of time, there was a good chance it would become about me and not *Suffra-Jette*.

Knowing that, I figured showing up right at six while the store was closed to get ready for the event would be safe. I didn't expect the entire parking lot to be blocked off by police barricades. Even with my windows closed, I can hear the loud pop music playing from a temporary stage on the other end of the lot. Food trucks and rows of plastic tables fill the pavement in front of the store.

Pressing the button that rolls down the window, I wait until it's all the way down and then wave to the officers chatting inside of the temporary barricades.

"Hi, gentlemen," I start. "I'm supposed to park out back in the employee lot, but I've never been here so I—"

"Isaac told us you'd be asking." One of them points to the other end of the building. "You're going to want to go to the far end. At the lights, take a right. There's a lot right behind the building. It's blocked off too, but just let them know who you are, and they'll let you in."

I nod and thank them, following his directions to the employee lot. At the back of the store, there's a glass door covered in flyers. In the middle of the door hangs a worn Employees Only sign. I assume that it's okay for me to let myself in. Zoe and Isaac are expecting me. My anxiety causes me to pause and second-guess myself, though.

What if it's not okay? What if I piss someone off? I'm just a guest in this world. I don't want to upset anyone, especially after Birdie's email last night. I should call Isaac and see where and when he wants me to come in.

"Are you just going to stand there all day?" an annoyed voice asks from behind me.

I turn to apologize, freezing in place when I see Birdie. Out of the big, fancy braid she had it in yesterday, Birdie's hair is now down, falling right below her chest, sleek and straight. She's wearing a black Stark Industries T-shirt and a pair of bright leggings covered in comic book onomatopoeias. I'm thankful my comic book knowledge allows me the insight that her shirt references Tony Stark of Iron Man's global tech company. Her makeup is bold tonight. Red and gold eyeshadow and long, thick black eyelashes create a dramatic look.

When I don't answer her or move out of the way, she raises her brows, unimpressed.

"Sorry," I apologize, opening the door and stepping back to hold it for her. "I just wasn't sure if I was allowed to go in."

She doesn't say a word as she walks past me. As much as I try my hardest to live up to my reputation of always being a gentleman, I am only human. Which is exactly why as soon as her back is fully to me, I take the chance to sneak a peek at her ass.

While I would say I'm a fan of the female body in its entirety, if I had to put some specific label on my appreciation, I would have to say I'm an ass man. I'll take a nice, firm ass over tits any day. And what I wouldn't give to take a bite outta Birdie's.

BIRDIE 8.

GOD, he's so infuriating. With his perfectly placed hair and his stupid dimples that make an appearance every time someone asks him to take a photograph. He's signed every little thing people have thrown at him, including a handful of arms for tattoos. There were a few women who tried to get him to sign their breasts. Even then, he said with such gracious ease that he was "flattered but didn't feel it was appropriate at a family-friendly event."

Everyone—but me—had agreed that Atticus should take the last seat at our table.

Francie winked. "Save the best for last."

Which wasn't a dig at me, the person that always sits last at our table during signings, but it stung like one anyway.

Campbell is the only one on our team that doesn't sit and sign the newest issue. There are a few diehard fans that will seek her out and ask to take photos with her, but it's always just been the six of us—Margot, Francie, Ramona, Nova, Zoe, and me. We all have our designated spots.

Readers know they're going to get me with my trademark gold Sharpie at the very end of the table.

But not today. Today, they get Atticus fucking Cohen and the boring black Sharpie he had to get from Isaac. I don't want him here, and why he needs to sign the issue is beyond me. He didn't contribute to it. Hell, he's not even Jette.

What's even more annoying is that he's so damn charismatic that I almost forget I hate him. Every time a little girl in a home-made Suffra-Jette costume comes up to the table, he pretends to be awestruck by her presence. Most of these girls have no idea who he is, but their mamas sure do.

Four hours after the first comic has been signed, Isaac locks the front door. I love getting the chance to talk to readers. I love being in the moment with them. But by the time ten o'clock rolls around, I'm ready to sit in a chair that doesn't make my butt go numb and eat the pizza Isaac and Bishop order after every monthly event.

Besides the team, the only people left are family members, including Isaac and Bishop and the store employees. Oh, and Atticus. He's still hanging around for some reason.

"Birdie! Mon bébé!" my mom calls out, waving her arms to get my attention from across the room.

It doesn't matter that I'm twenty-seven and surrounded by colleagues, Annie Yamamoto is going to make sure everyone in this room knows I'm her daughter. With the few seconds I have before ambush de Annie, I stretch my legs and wiggle my fingers.

I didn't keep track, but there were more people here tonight than there has been at any signing before.

We didn't even need the added draw of Atticus to pull people in.

Following suit after me, Atticus stands up and introduces himself to my parents, and I'm unprepared for how quickly they fall under his spell.

"You must be Mr. And Mrs. Yamamoto."

At the same time, both Atticus and my father extend their hands. Dad's posture is stiff and rigid. From the look of it, he squeezes Atticus's hand a little harder than necessary. Admittedly, the amount of pure joy it gives me is immature, but that joy dissipates the moment my mom refutes my dad's coldness with a warm, bubbly embrace.

"There's no need for formalities here." With open arms, Mom brushes off being called Mrs. Yamamoto immediately. "Annie and Ken are just fine. Right, dear?"

Even growing up, she was never Mrs. Yamamoto to any of my friends. When I was little, I remember her being called Mrs. Annie, but as I grew older and my friend circle became consistent, and albeit smaller, all of my friends just called her Momma Annie.

It's what Campbell, her brother, Cash, the women of the *Suffra-Jette* team, and half the Coolidge Comics & Collectables staff call her to this day.

Smiling tightly, Dad notices Mom's cue and agrees with her, but the second Atticus and her are hugging, he rolls his eyes.

"Be good," I mouth.

There may be a room full of other people freaking out over Atticus's presence, but I can at least count on my dad to be Team Birdie.

As Atticus and my mom step away from each other, Atticus's eyes light up. A woman a little bit older than my parents approaches us. Her sleek stacked bob is a silvery gray. Her lips are painted bright red with lipstick. She's wearing a black T-shirt with Suffra-Jette's neon lightning bolt symbol. Simple black leggings and a pair of Adidas athletic shoes finish off her ensemble.

"Well, if it isn't my favorite gal." When she's close enough, Atticus leans over and presses his cheek to hers, and both of them make a kissing motion.

"You better not let Mila hear you say that," she teases.

Mila must be the mystery woman he was seen with a few weeks ago. The press got a glimpse of a woman in his car, but they couldn't make out who it was. I mean, not that I spiraled down a rabbit hole on the internet last night or anything.

"Before I get scolded for being rude," Atticus starts, stepping back slightly, "let me introduce my aunt Bea. Aunt Bea, this is Annie, Ken, and Birdie Yamamoto. Birdie is the—"

"Creator and writer of my favorite comic book." Bea opens her arms in a similar fashion to how my own mother did with Atticus a few minutes before. "I feel like I already know you from everything Atticus has told me."

Oh fuck. I wonder what story he chose to tell her. The one that ends with me being a fangirl sexualizing his half-naked body, or the one where I storm out of the room on some diva-level shit? Let's be real: neither option makes me look great.

Shifting nervously, I nod. There's something about this woman's presence that makes me feel smaller. I don't think it's intentional. The way she carries herself, head held high, shoulders back, isn't with the tiniest bit of arrogance.

Atticus's ability to command the attention of everyone in a room without trying is clearly a Cohen family trait.

"It's so nice to meet you," I tell her. "I promise I'm not as bad as he made me seem."

The scoff from Atticus pulls my attention away from his aunt. "I've done nothing but sing your praises, thank you very much."

His aunt confirms such, but I don't take too much stock in her assurance. I, too, have parental figures that would lie to cover my ass if necessary.

"So Atticus. My daughter tells me you're an actor, but I can't place seeing you in anything," my dad says, feigning interest in Atticus's career.

Shots fired.

That's a bold-faced lie. He knows exactly who Atticus is. Before yesterday's conversation in my parents' kitchen, he knew.

I mean, he may not have known him by name, but he absolutely could have pointed him out as the guy from *Sunset Heights*. And! Less than a month ago, we saw a war movie he was in with Leonardo DiCaprio and Timothée Chalamet.

"Well, I was in a primetime teen drama for most of my late teens." Atticus takes the dig in complete stride. "*Sunset Heights* probably wouldn't be your cup of tea, but rumor has it, Birdie watched it, so I was on your TV for years and you must not have known it."

A mischievous twinkle dances about in his blue eyes as he references one of the most humiliating moments of my entire life.

"*Sunset Heights!*" Mom gushes with recognition. "Birdie, you and Campbell loved that show."

It doesn't surprise me that he's managed to bamboozle her. Dad will be a tougher cookie to crack, for sure, but now isn't the time or the place.

Turning to Atticus's aunt, I ask, "Do you still live in New England?"

AFTER ATTICUS'S RED SOX REMARK YESTERDAY, THIS topic of small talk may be the safest spot we have right now.

"I do!" she says. "In the very same house Atticus grew up in Concord."

"New Hampshire or Massachusetts?" my mom asks. "I only ask because I grew up in Lexington. My parents still live there."

"What a small world. Massachusetts." Both women's eyes light up when they realize they have something in common. "Next time you're in the area, we should grab lunch. I have a feeling we'll be seeing a lot of each other while these two are working together. It would be nice to know a familiar face at these big events."

"I would love that," Mom says as she pulls her phone from her little Coach clutch. "What's your number?"

Bea Cohen rattles off the ten-digits as Atticus leans in, chuckling. "I'm pretty sure they just became best friends. And to think, *we* haven't even exchanged numbers yet."

"Isn't it funny how that works?" I give him a tight smile before excusing myself when I see Campbell followed by Cash, stacks of pizza boxes in his hands. "I'm going to go say hi to Campbell and Cash." Turning to Bea, I say, "It was so nice to meet you."

I've exhausted all my small talk, and the will to keep my professionalism intact while being around Atticus is slipping further and further away.

He's not the first guy to look down on me just because I'm a woman in this industry. He certainly won't be the last. And there's nothing I love more than proving men wrong.

ATTICUS 9.

THE FIRST DAY of filming is reminiscent of the first day of school. There's an overwhelming mix of jittery nerves and anticipation as I show the security guard my identification.

I'm supposed to be here, but until I get through the checkpoint, there's always some unexplainable paranoia that they're going to kick me out. I'm the same way at airports. I know I don't have any drugs or firearms on me, but I'm always ninety percent sure someone slipped a kilo of cocaine into the bag that's been right by my side.

Luckily, I make it through the security checkpoint without getting detained. While the table read was at a fancy hotel in Boston, most of the filming for *Suffra-Jette* will take place outside of the city in a studio. All of my time on the movie will be in the studio.

After an hour in hair and makeup and then another forty-five minutes in wardrobe, I head in the direction of Stage C. I don't get more than a few steps before a slew of small beeps sound behind me. I turn to see Isaac Adams driving a two-seater golf cart.

"Hey, handsome! Need a ride?" he asks, slowing down next to me. He pats the empty seat next to him and I take a seat. "Where we headed today?"

"Stage C," I tell him.

"Me too." He grins. "Zoe and the girls are already there."

And suddenly, my nerves intensify. After the signing last week, I'm certain Birdie Yamamoto hates me. I'm not even sure why. I've played back the night in my head over and over. She seems to have done a complete one-eighty since the table read.

I knew how important the event was to her. I tried to stay in the background as often as possible, only taking photos or signing things if asked. I didn't say anything that could have offended her. I was nice to her parents—not that being nice to them was hard.

Annie reminds me a lot of Aunt Bea. It was quite easy to see she would move heaven and earth for her daughter, and everyone in the room seemed to call her Momma Annie. Ken was a little tougher. I felt like I was under a microscope all night with him, but he was never rude in his constant questioning. Aunt Bea and I managed to get an invite to this weekend's monthly family dinner they have with Campbell's family. An invitation I accepted eagerly.

By the time Isaac and I walk onto set, the production crew is there and the entire *Suffra-Jette* team is sitting in personalized canvas director's chairs.

In a room full of people, she's the first one I see.

Birdie is in a long powder blue maxi dress covered in white flowers. Her hair is down in waves. She looks like she should be on the beach with a good book instead of being stuck inside on this gorgeous April day.

Today, we're on the set built to look like Jette and Otto's apartment. It reminds me of my sister's house—clean and bright, with decorative glass vases and expensive "look, don't sit on" furniture.

This scene is an emotional one: Jette just found out that Otto's father is the villain, and she's having a tough time controlling her electro-energy before telling him. It's already caused a power outage in their apartment, and Otto is doing his best to be supportive, even though he doesn't know what's wrong or what he can do to help.

"And go!" Haley cues from the side.

The scene begins with Otto chasing Jette from room to room, so I follow Violet as she moves about the apartment set.

"Babe, wait." I say my lines with as much anguish as I can imagine Otto feeling in this moment. "Please, stop. For just one second. You need to take—"

"Oh, for fuck's sake!"

The director yells, "Cut!" and I immediately search the set for the culprit of the outburst. The annoyance I feel dissipates as soon as I see Birdie with crossed arms and lips curled in a tight scowl. Her eyes narrow in on me as if I'm the villain here.

"I'm so sorry," she apologizes. Her cheeks instantly flush when she realizes every single person on set is now looking at her.

The way her eyes roll in my direction says otherwise.

"No, no, no." Haley waves her off. "I want to hear what you think. This is your baby."

"You really don't," Birdie mutters sheepishly.

"Oh, come on," Violet coaxes her from next to me. "Is it me? If it is, please tell me. Jette is your character. You know her better than anyone. Help me."

"It's not you. I promise," Birdie assures her. "I'm sorry. I won't interrupt again."

"So, it's me," I say, locking eyes with her. When she doesn't answer, I begin to walk off the apartment set toward where she's sitting. "Talk to me. Don't worry about anyone else. It's just you and me. Tell me what you need from me."

"I don't believe you," she says with such conviction. "I don't think you give a shit about anyone other than yourself."

"Are we talking about Otto? Because this seems personal. Did I do something to upset you, Birdie? If I did, I'm sorry. The last thing I want is to—"

Cutting me off, she shakes her head. "It doesn't matter."

"It matters to me," I tell her. But she shuts down, and I remember we're on set with dozens of people waiting.

Dropping my voice, I lean in so she's the only one that hears me. "This conversation isn't over."

Not waiting for her to counter argue, I head back to the bedroom set. The best thing to do right now is move on. Birdie won't open up to me when she thinks an entire production crew is watching her, but I'm more determined to find the underlying cause of Birdie's distaste for me. Maybe I can convince her to grab dinner… or coffee… but after I return to the apartment set, I quickly glance over and see Birdie's chair sitting empty.

ATTICUS 10.

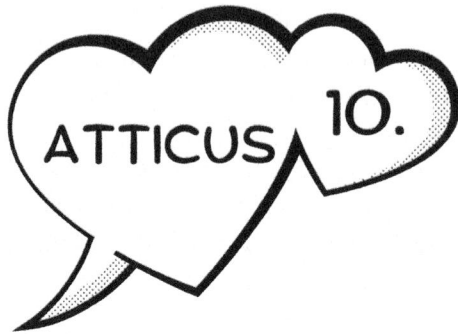

"OKAY, OKAY. I'M UP." I shake my head at the massive gray paw thumping against my chest before my eyes even open. I turn to look at the clock on my nightstand. When I see that it isn't quite six, I sigh. "Oh, Parker. You couldn't have let me sleep until the sun rose?"

At the sight of me sitting up, my sixty-pound husky's tail wags ferociously. With ease, he stretches lazily and jumps off the bed. Before I manage to slide both feet into my slippers, he makes his way around to me.

I'm not naïve enough to presume that caring for a human child is remotely close to taking care of a dog, but being Parker's dad certainly has provided me many, many early mornings. The husky, despite having his own full-size bed in his own room, spends about every night in bed with me. The trainer insisted I lay rules down, but all it took was one thunderstorm of him howling in fear for me to share my space with him. I went from a queen-size bed to a California king. I know if I ever get serious with someone there will have to be some major adjustments to the sleeping arrangements, but I figure I'll deal with that when the time comes. For now, I'm more than happy to share my sleeping space with him.

I may have rescued Parker from the shelter, but he rescued me in every other sense of the word. They say love at first sight isn't real, but I knew I was taking him home the moment I laid eyes on him. My niece was volunteering at the local shelter for the day and forgot her lunch. My sister called, knowing I was home, and asked me to run something over to her. I dropped off a turkey and cheese sandwich and brought home a one-year-old husky.

The shelter manager expedited the process knowing who I was. On any other given day, I would have all but demanded they make no special exception for me, but getting Parker off that cold cement floor felt more important than staying humble. Luckily, I knew a few people with huskies, so after just a few phone calls, I had a shopping list of things to get for my new bud. Before the day was done, Parker had everything he needed and then some.

I pull out the container filled with his homemade food, open the lid, and then drop three cups into a bowl. While he's devouring the ground turkey, quinoa, and veggies, I make my first cup of coffee.

I'm not scheduled on set today, but I check my phone just in case something changed. And I'm glad I do. Turns out, about an hour ago, I got a text from Campbell asking me to meet her at the *Suffra-Jette* team's trailer to "talk about the situation with Birdie."

Birdie never returned to the set yesterday. Zoe made an excuse for her. I'm not even going to pretend to understand what's going on anymore. I will, however, take a helping hand extended my way. So, after a quick run around the block with Parker, I shower and head to the studio.

Their trailer is about a dozen trailers away from mine and a hell of a lot smaller. Which doesn't make much sense considering there are six of them and just one of me. After rapping my knuckles on the door, I'm surprised when it opens and I'm greeted by a scowling Birdie. With crossed arms and narrowed eyes, it's apparent she's not thrilled to see me.

"This is a terrible idea," she says, shaking her head as I make my way inside.

"Quiet down and close the door," Campbell reprimands. "And it is not a terrible idea. In fact, it's one of my most brilliant. Good morning, Atticus. Coffee?"

"Please," I say, despite just finishing a cup at home. "I have a feeling I'm going to need it."

"Might want to give him the vodka too," Birdie mutters.

"I have a feeling I might regret asking, but what's going on?" Taking the cup of coffee from Campbell, I thank her, my eyes darting between the two women in the room in search of some kind of hint as to what I just walked into.

"Okay." Campbell takes a breath, her shoulders rising and falling on the exhale. "I know you're not big on the whole social media thing, so you probably didn't see, but you and Miss Sunshine over here are trending. Someone—we're not sure who yet—leaked to the press that she"—Campbell points to Birdie—"hates you." She points to me. "And now people from all sides of it are fighting. Fans of Birdie's. Fans of yours. There's a lot of finger-pointing and blame for something that is a complete nonissue."

I'm no stranger to the media and the way they distort information to fit whatever narrative they're trying to sell. Tabloids spew bullshit in hopes of grabbing people's attention in the grocery store check-out line. And everyone has a camera right in their phone these days. I've never had to deal with that here, though. In Los Angeles, sure, and the few times I've filmed in London, but never at home in New England.

I've always found a way to blend in. A pair of sunglasses, a Red Sox hat, and plain clothing, always.

"What are you suggesting we do to combat it?" I ask before taking a sip of my coffee.

"Alright, so," she begins, "there's a group of fans—both yours and Birdie's alike—that are convinced you're an item. There's a photo of you two in a stare down, and they're saying that there's no way you two"—she hands me her phone to show me—"aren't fucking. They think the drama on set was to throw everyone off to keep your relationship a secret."

"Is that why you've been acting like you hate me?" I ask, catching a glimpse of Birdie just in time to see her rolling her eyes. "If you've been harboring feelings for me, now might be a good time to fess up."

I know she doesn't like me, and now the rest of the world knows too, but this is what we needed to happen to work through this. We're going to be a part of each other's lives for at least a year. It would be much easier for everyone involved if Birdie and I could just get along.

Birdie sighs. "Someone has clearly watched one too many rom-coms. As if anyone would *genuinely* believe the two of us would be together."

I've sat through her little jabs and the daggers she's tried to shoot out of her eyes, but enough is enough. I've been nothing but nice to her—gone out of my way to make sure she knew how much I respected her and the story she created. I haven't done anything wrong.

"What happened to the girl before the table read?" I question, turning my attention to Birdie specifically. "Where did she go? I'm not expecting you or anyone else to kiss my ass, but obviously something changed here."

"You can't be serious." She scoffs, looking back and forth between me and Campbell. "Okay, picture this. It's after the table read. I'm standing there like a fucking idiot, holding those comics you brought. I sign every single one of them, and when I take them over to you, I decide I'm also going to invite you to grab lunch later in the week, because it *seemed* like you love this series, and I would have loved to hear your ideas for Otto. Then, I get the pleasure of hearing how you think this entire thing is a feminist stunt and that you only offered to make up for Violet's salary with your own because it would look good in the headlines."

Before I can wrap my head around what she's saying, Campbell bursts out in laughter.

"Anyone else!" Birdie snaps at Campbell. "I would have been okay with *anyone else* getting sucked up into this bullshit. But *you're* supposed to be my best friend."

Whipping her body around with so much force I'm slightly surprised she doesn't topple over, Birdie makes her way toward the trailer door.

As her words begin to sink in, it hits me. This has been a terrible misunderstanding. But that also means it's fixable.

I can fix this.

I just have to get Birdie to stay and listen long enough to realize it too.

"No, Birdie, wait," I call out. With one hand on the door, she pauses. Her back is still to us as I begin to explain what really happened at the table read. "You missed the part where Campbell asked me if I would do an interview with Pow! Press, and I said no because my agent had already set up an interview with Jason Franco."

She turns back to face me. Her arms are crossed, her brows pinched in suspicion. I'm not in the clear yet, but she's still here. A small victory is still a victory.

"Okay, and?" she questions, looking back and forth between Campbell and me.

"The entire time we were on the call, *he* was the one suggesting and pushing me to admit all that," I tell her.

Her shoulders rise and fall as she inhales and exhales, closing her eyes as she winces. "I'm an idiot."

"No, you're not," I assure her. "I would hate me too. But for the record, *I* never thought any of that. That's the narrative the magazine was pushing. Not me. Every bit of excitement I had —*have*—is genuine."

"I don't expect you to understand, but as a woman in a male-driven industry, there's so much riding on this movie. This could open the door for so many other small, independent comics— especially those with a female-led arc," she explains. "No matter what happens with this movie, you'll land another role. This might be the last time I'm ever on a movie set, Atticus. All of that aside, *Suffra-Jette* is just so damn important to me. When I thought you took the role as a publicity stunt, I felt like you were making fun of me, of everything I stand for. Especially after you came into the table read asking me to sign your comics."

"Which is *why* I think you should give the people what they want," Campbell interjects. "I know this movie means a lot to both of you. You and Birdie should date. Or pretend to, at least. Think of it as a salvage tactic. We need to drum up some good publicity."

I don't take the time to think about all the reasons why it wouldn't work, and immediately say yes.

Turning to Birdie, I shrug. "I want what's best for the movie. You want what's best for the movie. What do we have to lose?"

As soon as Atticus agrees to it, I know there's no choice other than going along with Campbell's crazy idea. I still don't think it's going to work, though. Atticus is cut from the cloth of a god. He's a walking talking orgasm waiting to happen. I think that's part of the reason I was so pissed when I thought that he was using *Suffra-Jette* for "feminist" publicity. I thought we had been duped. That *I* had been duped.

Turns out, I'm just an asshole who jumps to conclusions and he *really* is perfect. So, there's that.

But the point still stands: as much as people say that looks don't matter, they do. And on any given day, I'm okay being the girl that has a little extra junk in her trunk. Because as much as I love hiking, I also love pizza. With my writing schedule, the chances of me getting pizza delivered are much higher than having the time to head to the mountains for the day. I do my best to make sure I stay as active as I can when I have to be stuck at my desk. I drink all my water. And I mean, sure, I could eat a salad instead of fettucine alfredo for lunch. But to be honest... I just don't want to.

So there's me. Curves for days; a little extra here and there. Not to mention, generally speaking, I'm awkward as fuck. I have anxiety and ADHD—which is a super fun combination. Hyperfocusing and then spiraling down into endless rabbit holes is my least favorite pastime, yet it seems to be the thing I do the most. My brain doesn't ever stop. Even when I take medication, the part of me that worries to the point of feeling like my heart is going to pound out of my chest doesn't simply go away.

And that's why as soon as I decided Atticus was a piece of shit, that was it. He just was. My stubbornness and pride may have also played a role in that too. The hyperfixating is also why I spent two hours on my laptop trying to find out everything I could about Atticus after I left the set yesterday.

Much to my dismay at the time, the guy's a saint. He has a little bit of a player past while in his teen and early twenties, but since he turned twenty-four, he's only dated one other person publicly. There are all the basic things, like his favorite color *(blue)*, his favorite food *(his aunt's baked mac and cheese),* and his favorite sports team *(The Red Sox)*, but I also read an interview where he talked about his favorite book *(The Giver)* and how many hours of sleep he needs to function properly *(at least six)*.

I feel like I already know him. And what I do know is that guys like Atticus don't go for girls like me. Atticus's own past would suggest that he would *never* date me. Everyone he's been connected to has been brunette like me, but an actor and athletically built. I may have also stalked the last three of them on social media. I'm not proud of myself, but what's done is done.

"Do you have any plans for the rest of the day?" Atticus asks before taking a sip of his coffee. I'm sure the generic K-cups we have are beneath his normal cup of joe, but he doesn't seem to mind. "We should spend some time together. *Get our stories straight* kind of thing. I'm not on the call sheet at all today, so I've got some time."

"I rode in with Campbell," I tell him. It's not really an excuse, but I can't exactly take off with her car and leave her stranded on set.

"I can take you home to get your car," he suggests. "Or just drop you off at home later. It's a gorgeous day. We could head into the city if you want." Pausing, he looks at Campbell. "I'm sure Boston is the place to go if we want to get captured on camera."

Campbell grabs her bag from the little pull-down table in our kitchenette. "It sounds like my work here is done. I will see *you*" —she pauses to look at me—"back at the house later. And I will see *you*"—another pause to look at Atticus—"on Sunday."

Oh shit. I forgot my parents invited Atticus and his aunt to family dinner. The Porter and Yamamoto families have been doing Sunday dinner together for as long as I can remember. When Cash, Campbell, and I went away to college and started our own lives, it became difficult to get together every week. So, our parents made us promise that the first weekend of every month, we would always have dinner with them.

"I guess we're spending the day together, then," I say.

The severity of what we're about to do suddenly weighs heavy on me. Are we going to tell our friends? Our family? I don't know if I can lie to my parents.

"Don't worry," he says as he places his coffee cup down. "We've got all day to figure it out."

"Huh? What?" I try to brush off my anxiety.

It doesn't work internally, but if I can just act calm enough so Atticus doesn't realize I'm losing my shit over here, that would be swell.

"I'm freaking out a bit too." His lips curl into a smirk. "But I think it'll be fun. We'll make it fun. I promise."

ATTICUS 12.

I HAVEN'T BEEN to the New England Aquarium since I was a kid. I'm not sure why it was the first place to pop into mind when Birdie asked if I had a plan or if we were just going to wander around the city until someone saw us together.

The woman at the ticket counter recognized me immediately. Normally, I would cringe at the thought of the special attention, but the way Birdie's eyes lit up when Janet—according to her name tag—asks if we would like a private tour of the penguin exhibit, I can't bring myself to decline.

"What do you think, hon?" I ask, trying out 'hon' and regretting it the moment the word left my lips.

Nope. Birdie isn't a "hon," and not a "honey" either.

"I would love that," she admits.

"Well, there you go." I turn back to Janet. "We would love to."

Janet smiles, her eyes darting back and forth between me and Birdie like she's trying to figure out our relationship.

Given the circumstances, keeping as many people as possible in the dark about this is for the best.

"Morgan, our penguin aquarist, is currently in the middle of a tour, but if you meet back here in a half hour, she can take you down to the exhibit," Janet says. "If you need anything until then, just ask anyone in a blue collared shirt."

I thank her, sliding my hand into Birdie's as we walk away. There's a stiffness at first, but when I lean in and whisper, "If we want people to think we're a couple, we have to act like one," her fingers loosen and wrap around mine.

"I used to love coming here as a kid," I tell Birdie. "My mom would bring me and my sister on school vacations."

"You have just the one?" she asks, clarifying before I can answer. "Sister. Just the one sister. I know you have just one mom. Or, had. Oh God. I'm done talking now."

Chuckling, I nod. "Yes. Just the one sister. Her name is Eliza. She's married to her college boyfriend, Quincy, and they have two daughters, Mila and Emma. They still live in Lexington. How about you? Any siblings?"

Birdie fills me in about her life as we walk hand in hand. Occasionally, I look over my shoulder. I'm used to feeling like someone is watching me, but with Birdie by my side, I'm hyper-aware of my surroundings today.

When she stops short to look at a turtle swimming by in the floor-to-ceiling tank, I notice a woman with bleach blonde hair staring at us. As soon as I make eye contact, she looks away and turns around.

I think we've been caught.

Which would normally annoy me, but that is the whole purpose of this little outing, isn't it?

I'm about to tell Birdie, but she sighs happily, stilling for a moment as she looks up at me. "Did Campbell tell you?"

"Tell me what?" I ask. Granted, Campbell has told me a lot of things, but I don't think it's whatever Birdie is referring to.

"That bringing me around animals would make me happy," she says, looking forward into the tank again.

"No, but that's good to know for future reference," I say, making a mental note. "Do you have any animals?"

"Unless you count the birds I feed and the rabbits and deer that visit in the spring, no." She pauses again when an eel swims past us. "You have a dog, right?"

"How very Snow White of you," I tease. "I do. Parker is a two-year-old husky."

"Parker? As in Peter?" she asks, shrugging when my brows quirk at her incredibly specific guess. "What? I did my homework."

"So you Googled me?" I tease, giving her hand a gentle squeeze. "Don't worry. I Googled you too."

"You did?"

"Oh yeah." I chuckle at her disbelief. There's no shame in my game. I haven't felt the need to see what the internet is saying about me in a long time, but I don't doubt Birdie's search led her to things well beyond the editorial pieces I found on her. "You made *30 Under 30* last year, huh? Impressive."

"I don't know if you're making fun of me or not."

I can feel her eyes boring into me as if the truth lies somewhere inside me.

"Not even a little bit," I tell her honestly before switching gears. Getting to know her has been fun, but if we're going to make this fake relationship work, we're going to have to figure out the technicalities. "So, this thing with us. Are you going to tell your parents? Your dad scares me a little, and I need to know what I'm walking into on Sunday."

At that, Birdie lets out something resembling a cackle, followed by louder laughter. Her body shakes as she covers her mouth.

"I'm sorry," she starts. "That's my fault. I went to my parents' house after the table read and…"

"Oh man." I groan, shaking my head. "So your dad thinks I'm a giant piece of shit. Cool, cool."

"We can tell them that we talked?" she suggests as we approach the front desk. Janet waves at us and lets us know that Morgan will be here soon. After I thank her, Birdie continues. "And when we did, I don't know, we realized there was some kind of connection? I hate the thought of lying to them, but my mom would disclose information to someone unintentionally."

"I may tell my sister, but I won't be telling Aunt Bea," I admit. "I love her, but she's not exactly the best secret keeper either. I do think Isaac and Zoe should know."

"So, our friends know the truth, but we're conning our family and the rest of the world." Birdie lets out a breath. "Got it."

BiRDiE 13.

MAYBE BEING Atticus's pretend girlfriend won't be so bad. If the time we spend together is anything like what it's been like so far, I can even see a real, genuine friendship coming from this.

While we wait for Morgan to arrive, we cover all general bases of our fake relationship. Dates in public once a week if Atticus's filming schedule allows for it. Minimal time together with our families—neither of us wants anyone to get too attached. Though we both agreed that if my parents or Aunt Bea initiate plans, we'll have to follow through with them. We'll tell the *Suffra-Jette* team the truth—I'll tell the girls and Atticus will take care of telling Isaac and Nova's husband, Bishop. I told him he wouldn't have to since Zoe and Nova will find out, but he insisted anyway.

"Speaking of everyone, do you have any plans tomorrow night?" Atticus asks, lowering his voice as a petite blonde steps up to the front desk and talks to Janet.

As the two of them speak in hushed tones, looking over at Atticus and I occasionally, my stomach twists. Walking around with him, it was easy to get lost in conversation, losing sight of the fact that we were drawing attention to ourselves the entire time just by being here. There's no going back now.

"I know it's last minute," he says," but there's a charity gala I have to attend. We could go together. Isaac, Zoe, Bishop, and Nova will be there too, so you'll have people there with you if I have to socialize. I can get tickets for Ramona, Francie, and Campbell too. The *Suffra-Jette* team can have their own table."

My initial instinct is to make an excuse not to go.

Being here, in a public setting with Atticus, is nerve-racking enough, but something like a gala would be shining a spotlight on our "relationship."

By industry standards, I'm well known in the comic book world. Walking around conventions, I get recognized and asked for selfies or to sign copies of *Suffra-Jette*, but I can walk out my front door and no one really knows or cares who I am. I can go grocery shopping without people trying to take my photograph. I know the second the world realizes this "thing" with Atticus is real—or as real as we're trying to make them believe it is—all of that is going to change.

But if I don't do it tomorrow, it'll be some other time, and the whole point of this is to spin the bad press, right? What better way to spin it than by showing up together for a charity event? And my friends will be there. How bad could it really be?

"Talk about ripping off the Band-Aid." I concede to the idea. God, I wish he wouldn't look at me like he can see right through my façade of being perfectly fine with all of this. "Okay, yes. I'm in. We should tell everyone about us sooner than tomorrow, though. And are you sure it's okay that I come? I know these things are planned out months in advance, and getting tickets for the girls? I don't want to ruffle any feathers when we're trying to prove to the world that I'm not an asshole."

"Did I mention that it's for The New England Academy for Young Arts?" Atticus grins as the blonde woman from the desk begins making her way over to us. "It's the art school my aunt teaches at and I attended. My sister is the one that puts together the gala every year. She always tells me to bring friends. That's how Isaac and Bishop got on the list. I called in a favor, and Isaac donated some amazing comic books for the silent auction."

"What time is all of this?" A jolt of panic sends crippling anxiety through me when I realize I don't have anything to wear to a charity gala as Atticus Cohen's date. "Because, um, I work from home, sooo, uh, my wardrobe is graphic tees and yoga pants. I don't have anything I could wear to something like that. I'll need to go shopping."

"I'll take care of everything," Atticus says before he gives my hand a reassuring squeeze. "Just say yes. Say you'll come."

Morgan is now close enough I can read her name tag, confirming she is in fact our tour guide.

Her voice shakes when she says hello and introduces herself. "Hi, I'm Morgan. I heard you want to see the penguins?"

"We would love to see them. Thank you so much for taking the time out of your day to give us a tour," Atticus says to her, his hand still firmly in mine as we begin to follow her into the penguin habitat.

"This is actually feeding time, so if you want to—and don't mind touching fish—we can even get you in there to feed a few."

The smallest gasp escapes my lips as I glance up to Atticus before turning to Morgan. "Can we really? Oh my gosh. This is officially the best date *ever*."

At that, Morgan's shoulders fall with ease as she begins her story about how many penguins are at the aquarium. As Atticus and I follow her lead into the habitat, I hang on to every bit of information she's giving to us.

"I have to know," Atticus starts. "The whole rock engagement thing and mating for life… Is that real?"

"This isn't exactly the kind of information we give on the standard tour, but yes and no," Morgan says. "Sure, some penguins—Galapagos penguins, for example—practice monogamy and return to their mate. But there are also plenty of studies that show other breeds, like the Adélies penguins from the Antarctic Peninsula, have resorted to a form of prostitution."

"Stop it!" I exclaim. "You're telling me I've lived the last twenty-seven years of my life without knowing about *penguin prostitution?*"

Not skipping a beat, she introduces us to Mike, another member of the penguin team who has joined us. Morgan grabs a bucket of fish and continues to tell us about how some females will find younger, inexperienced males. Then, they lure them with sex to gain access to the pebbles needed to build the walls that protect their egg-filled nests from being washed away.

"They look for the younger, single male penguins who have nothing but time to find pebbles. After they're, uh, done, the female stashes a pebble in her beak and goes back to add it to her own nest."

Atticus hasn't said a word this entire conversation, but while I've been squealing when one of the penguins waddles over to us or asking Morgan questions about penguin prostitution rings, he's had his eyes locked on me, the same amused half grin on his face the entire time.

"And on that note," Morgan says as two aquarium workers carrying two more big buckets join us in the aquarium, "it's lunchtime!"

BiRDiE 14.

THE NEW ENGLAND ACADEMY FOR YOUNG ARTS is the kind of high school I would have thrived in. The private school for the artistically gifted has multiple programs ranging from acting, graphic design, and music-based courses.

And its annual spring fundraiser hosted by the Cohen family is important. Many New-England-based celebrities secure invitations, but those that don't—or those from outside the region—are more than welcome to attend for a small ticket price of twenty-five thousand dollars.

It's like the Met Gala. Just in Boston. There's a theme every year, and a silent auction, but I already knew all of this before Atticus tried to bring me up to speed on the drive to my house last night.

All the who's who in New England royalty attend this fundraiser. From fellow Hollywood stars like Chris Evans, the Wahlberg brothers, and Adam Sandler to musicians like Steven Tyler of Aerosmith and the Dropkick Murphys. And I know next to nothing about sports, but even I recognized the names of all the Boston sports legends Atticus said would be in attendance.

As Atticus promised, his assistant, Diane, texts me at seven o'clock in the morning on the dot, letting me know that not only will tickets for me and the girls, *and* plus ones for each of them, be delivered to my house but that he also arranged for transportation for them. I assumed I would be going with the girls, until I got a follow-up text saying that Atticus will be here to pick me up at four o'clock this afternoon. Which will be fine—except I still don't know what I'm supposed to wear tonight.

I'm debating this when the doorbell chimes shortly before eight.

A man holding a small signature device smiles politely when I open my front door. "Are you"—he looks down at the name tag— "Birdie Yamamoto or Campbell Porter?"

I nod, stifling a yawn. "I'm Birdie."

"Perfect. Will you sign for these?" he asks, pointing down to the four boxes on the steps to the side of him.

Two at a time, I bring the boxes to the kitchen table. There are two with my name on them and two with Campbell's. Opening the big box first, I gasp when I see the little piece of white cardstock:

"The fairest in all the land. See you tonight, Snow White. – A."

The pink floral-printed sleeveless chiffon gown is something I never would have picked for myself. It's delicate, feminine, and the Millie Bradley label tells me it cost Atticus more than a month's rent for the condo.

Owning a Millie Bradley dress has been on my vision board since Campbell suckered me into making one with her last New Year's Eve. We're real party animals. We also shared about a hundred dollars in Chinese takeout and an entire box of wine. Because we're *also* classy as fuck.

Campbell yawns, joining me in the kitchen. "What's that?"

"I think Atticus sent us dresses for tonight," I tell her, still trying to wrap my head around the fact that I currently have a dress in my hands. "Campbell, this is a Millie Bradley."

Her eyes perk up immediately. "Us? As in *both* of us? I knew he was going to send you something, but I didn't expect him to send me something too."

Well, *that* snapped her out of her sleepy trance faster than I've ever seen a cup of coffee do. Gently pulling out the rest of my dress, I find myself sighing dreamily.

"Holy hell, B. It's…"

"Gorgeous?" I offer. "I know. And look at this."

Handing her the card with his note on it, I pull out a chair and take a seat before opening the smaller of the boxes.

"Snow White?" she questions. "You already have pet names for each other? It's been less than a day. I can't even with this cuteness."

"Cam." I know trying to reason with her is futile, but I try anyway.

Campbell is a hopeless romantic. If she's not working, she's watching shows like *Say Yes to the Dress* or reading a romance novel. There are a lot of things Campbell loves, like her job, her brother, her parents, singing off-key very loudly in the shower, and love. Campbell loves love. Her favorite holiday is Valentine's Day, whether she has a boyfriend or not. It's going to be hard to keep her thinking realistically when it comes to me and Atticus. I can already see the wheels spinning in her head as she tries to figure out how to make this *really* work between us.

The iridescent gold Christian Louboutin leather pumps in a size seven and a half in her hand seem to do the trick momentarily, though. *Thank you, Atticus.*

"Read mine," she says, handing me the note she pulled from one of her boxes.

"Best friends get the princess treatment too! – A."

"I figured he was up to something when he started pumping me for info at eleven o'clock last night, but man, oh man, I was not expecting this." Campbell picks up one of the shoes and grins. "He's good."

It doesn't surprise me that Campbell was in on this little surprise. It does surprise me that Atticus went to such lengths to figure out my dress and shoe size. For all I know, this could be very on par for him, though. I'm the one that decided I hated him based on a partial misheard conversation without even talking to him or anyone else about it.

After yesterday, I can confirm that it was just me jumping to conclusions.

Despite our best efforts, we left the aquarium smelling like fish, so sitting down in a restaurant for dinner was out of the question. We both had a good laugh when we revealed our Google search history on each other while trying to figure out if we could hit a drive-through on the way to my house.

"You need somewhere that has vegetarian options, right?" he asked, scrolling on his phone.

"Yep," I confirm. "And you're pescatarian?"

We opted for Pressed Café to go. Which was fine by me. It's one of my favorites, and Atticus had never been. The moan of approval when he took a bite of his smoked salmon bagel was all I needed to know it wouldn't be the last time we got food from there. Well, that and Atticus said so himself.

He gave me control of the music, handing me his phone without giving it a second thought. I chose to shuffle through his music library and properly embarrassed myself when I got more excited than I should at finding multiple songs by Sammy Rae & The Friends, my favorite band. The freak-out continued internally when he joined me in singing every single word of "Jackie Onassis."

I know more about him than I know about some of the people I've had in my life for years now. Most of what's on the internet is true: the good stuff, anyway. We didn't get into his past relationships—or mine either for that matter—but from what I can tell, what you see is what you get with Atticus. "Oh, and apparently, hair and makeup will be here at noon." Campbell grins, looking down at her phone for a moment before turning to show me the text from Atticus sitting on her home screen.

Atticus Cohen: *I have hair and makeup coming to your house at noon. I told them to expect two to five people. I don't have Ramona, Francie, or Margot's numbers, but this includes them.*

"I think this fake relationship is going to work out nicely for all of us."

Her verbiage makes me chuckle a bit, considering I thought the exact thing to myself when Atticus and I were at the aquarium yesterday. There's a lot to wrap my head around, but the one thing I know is that I need to call Atticus. Right now. No matter what arrangement we made for the benefit of the movie, he needs to know that I don't expect anything like this, ever.

Getting a private tour of the New England Aquarium was incredible, and having a gorgeous dress to wear tonight certainly makes my life a lot easier, but at the end of the day, these are the kinds of things you arrange for a girlfriend. A *real* girlfriend.

Campbell would tell me to just roll with it, but I can't. So, before calling him, I get up from the table, making the excuse I'd better go shower.

I don't even get over the threshold before my phone rings in my hand, and Ramona's name pops up on my screen.

"Mornin'," I answer, and I'm immediately greeted by a high-pitched scream.

"A currier just showed up to my front door with two very large white boxes." She squeals. "And inside those boxes was a gorgeous Prada dress and shoes! *Prada*, Birdie!"

Three little beeps in my ear signal another call coming through, so I look, unsurprised by the fact that it's Francie.

"Listen, Francie is calling me. Why don't you just head this way now? I'll explain everything when you get here."

"Be there in an hour. Love you, bye!" she says before we end the call, and then I have the same conversation with Francie. I completely understand their inability to wrap their heads around what's going on. Hell, I have no idea at this point, and it's happening to me.

Which reminds me, I still need to call Atticus.

It'll have to wait until after I get out of the shower, though. We're about to have a house full of women who are going to need to get ready for a night out. And I also need to call my parents. I can only imagine how upset my mom would be to find out about me and Atticus on the internet.

This just got real. Which is ironic considering it's all pretend.

"Go blast Sammy Rae, and use the lavender body scrub," Campbell says, breaking my thoughts. Looking around the kitchen counter, she shuffles the piles of junk mail until she finds her car keys. "I'm going to grab some celebratory cookies from White Wrapper."

"Okay... but what exactly are we celebrating?" I ask, really hoping she isn't celebrating this thing with Atticus.

Admittedly, I got swept up in it for a second. The dresses, the fact that he arranged for hair and makeup, and that he kept his word when he told me he'd take care of everything... It's all certainly swoonworthy, but it's just for show. This benefits him just as much as it does me, if not more. I'm not the one who has a contract for a bonus based on movie sales.

It's crazy how much has changed in the last twenty-four hours. I went from wanting to punch the man in his perfect smile to wanting to... No. No. We are not even going there. I cannot entertain those thoughts. This is business. We're business partners. One partner should not thank the other in the form of kissing the aforementioned perfect smile off their face.

Damn it. This is not good.

"We're celebrating you." Campbell shrugs. "Our team. *Suffra-Jette*. Since when do we need a legit reason for cookies? Go shower, hater. You have a hot date tonight."

AT EXACTLY FOUR O'CLOCK, the sound of the doorbell lets us know our ride is here. With each ring, my anxiety begins to manifest in a multitude of physical responses.

An accelerated pulse has me seriously questioning the likeliness of my heart slamming out of my chest. I count *one, two, one, two* to remind myself to breathe.

The second Campbell opens the front door, every little trick my therapist has ever taught me is gone, as if Hermione Granger herself is in our house. You know what doesn't obliviate, though? My nerves. In fact, they've intensified tenfold since Atticus stepped inside.

"Our hero," Campbell greets him, and I know it's only a matter of seconds until he's up the stairs to where the rest of us wait.

When he steps off the staircase, I have to remind myself to breathe again.

The bright navy suit and mint green shirt combination—much like my dress—is something I never would have chosen, but fuck does he pull it off. His hair is styled, and his facial hair is just slightly more cleaned up than it was when we saw each other yesterday. As he closes the space between us, the warm, woodsy tones of his cologne are intoxicating.

I've never used the word "swagger" seriously before now, but Atticus Cohen exudes swagger and BDE.

Swagger and big dick energy. That's Atticus Cohen, ladies and gents.

"And if it isn't the fairest one of all," he says softly when he reaches me. "Hi, Snow. You look beautiful."

"If I'm Snow White, then you're definitely Prince Charming."

Francie rattles off something about how the prince from Snow White is *actually* known as "The Prince" and Prince Charming is from Cinderella, but I'm only half listening as Atticus offers me his arm.

"Shall we?" he asks.

Be cool, Birdie. Do not imply that you would like to go to the bedroom and see what's under that perfectly tailored suit.

When we step outside, there are two limousines waiting for us.

"Sorry I didn't give you the heads-up I was coming," he says lowly before turning to the girls. "I figured it would make the most sense for me and Birdie to show up together since there will be press on the red carpet."

"Whatever you say, boss," Francie says with a wave as she dips down into the second limo. "This is your world, Atticus. We're just tagging along for Birdie."

I give a little wave to my friends before getting into our ride.

"I have a surprise for you," Atticus says once we're settled in.

"I don't know if my head or heart can handle anything else, Atticus," I tell him. "You've already done so much—"

"Well, I know you had your heart set on 'This Is War' by Thirty Seconds to Mars for Jette's big fight scene at the end. I called in a favor…"

Tears brim in my eyes as he tells me how he did the friend-of-a-friend thing to connect with Jared Leto.

Swallowing, I look up to the roof of the limo, willing myself not to cry and mess up my makeup.

"I don't even know what to say," I admit. "I certainly don't deserve this after the way I treated you."

Brushing it off, Atticus smiles. "It was a misunderstanding... which you already apologized for."

"Thank you."

Two words. That's all I have in me. Fight or flight has kicked in, and I'm certain if this car weren't already in motion, I would run back inside the condominium and lock the doors behind me.

Yesterday was easy. Too easy. We got to enjoy each other's company and laugh over hooker penguins, and it gave me the delusional belief that I could handle something like this. I don't think I can do it. I'm going to blow this entire thing, and in doing so, ruin Atticus's career, my credibility, and the movie. My parents are going to hate me for lying to them.

Shit, my mom. Amid all the craziness, I didn't even get to call her.

"I need to call my mom." I swallow, wishing I brought a bottle of water as I pull my phone from my clutch bag. "I need to tell them something before all of this happens."

"Good call," Atticus agrees. "I already told my aunt and my sister. Eliza knows the truth. Aunt Bea is so excited to see my girlfriend tonight."

It didn't dawn on me until he said his sister's name that she would be there as well. I mean, I knew. He told me yesterday that she plans the event each year. Suddenly, being around all those big-name celebrities doesn't seem as intimidating. I'm about to walk straight into the lion's den. Atticus just reassured me that Eliza knows our relationship is a fabricated setup, but that doesn't seem to matter right now.

Even being around Aunt Bea is daunting. Despite having met

her already, it's different now. In her mind, I'm Atticus's new girl-friend. It's the people-pleasing side of me, but I just want them to like me. I can't explain why.

I'm about to be in the presence of the women that mean the most to Atticus, and suddenly the technicalities of our relation-ship—or lack thereof—mean nothing. I want them to like me. However, I know I have no right to expect that from them.

Just how long will we need to continue pretending, though? Are we expected to spend the holidays and our birthdays together? Filming will be wrapped by Christmas, but the movie isn't set to come out for at least a year. Then there will be press leading up to the release, the premiere...

"Hey," Atticus says, placing his hand on my thigh. I'm sure it's meant to be reassuring, but the jolt of adrenaline that courses through my body at his touch feels like a shock of electricity. It's too bad I can't harness that energy like Jette can. "We're going to kill this. And if all else fails, it's open bar. We'll just get drunk and have fun."

"I need to call my mom," I say again, wanting desperately to believe him.

"Alright." He nods, taking his hand from my thigh. "We got this. I promise you."

ATTICUS 16.

OUT OF ALL THE events I'm scheduled to attend each year, the fundraiser for the Academy of Arts is always my favorite. Even more so than movie premieres. Mostly because it's personal. The Academy provided my aunt with the income to take care of me and Eliza growing up, and it put me right on the path leading me to where I am today.

The fundraiser has become such an in-demand event that planning it became my sister's full-time job three years ago. The last few years have been incredible and have proven that Eliza is a miracle worker. From Cirque du Soleil to *the* Wayne Newton performing at the "Vegas, Baby!" themed fundraiser, she's put together amazing events.

This year's theme is Regency Modern, no doubt thanks to all the books Bea and Eliza have been reading over the past year after watching *Bridgerton*, the Netflix show based on historical romances written by Julia Quinn. I only know as much because dukes and balls were all they could talk about for weeks after it came out.

While I'm sure there will be a corset or tall-standing coat collar amongst the guests, it certainly isn't required. Just elegance, extravagance, and high society—perfect for Hollywood in Massachusetts.

Birdie handles the red carpet like a pro. If it weren't for her tight grip on my hand, I never would have guessed this is her first time at an event like this.

"You did amazing," I whisper once we've gotten past the line of press and into the building.

Men in suits direct us to a beautiful empty ballroom.

"Where is everyone?" Campbell asks from behind us.

"Outside," I answer, pointing ahead to the open doors that lead to the gardens. "Eliza chose Higgins House because of its gardens and because it has space if Mother Nature decided she didn't want to play nice today."

"Good evening!" The trumpeter greets us as we step forward, following one of the Jonas Brothers and his wife. "How would you like to be announced?"

My answer earns me a small laugh from Birdie and the girls.

"Ready?" I ask, looking down at Birdie.

"As I'll ever be."

Stepping forward, we wait until the trumpet finishes his call and then begin to make our way into the gardens.

"Presenting Miss Birdie Yamamoto," the trumpeter calls out. "Escorted by The Right Honorable Lord Atticus Cohen."

I had an idea of what to expect walking out here—my sister and Aunt Bea have been texting me photos all day—so when I hear the small intake of Birdie's breath, I glance over just in time to catch her reaction.

"Atticus, this is..." Her eyes widen with every step we take. "This must be a dream."

The grandeur of the event is in the bouquets of long-stemmed pink and white tulips scattered on high-top tables around a temporary dance floor. Food and drink stations feature gourmet macaroons, fresh fruits, hand-squeezed lemonades, and sparkling mineral water imported from Italy.

We don't have a moment of time to ourselves before my aunt and sister make their way to us.

"You must be the infamous Birdie." Eliza lowers her voice as she pulls Birdie into a hug. "Since you two are dating, I'm going to hug you tightly now because I'm sure the rest of the world assumes there's *no way* tonight would be the first time we've met. I want everyone to think I adore you."

"I want everyone to think the feeling is mutual," Birdie says as she and Eliza hug.

My aunt pulls Birdie into her arms next, and the warm rush of emotion as I see the three of them acting like the best of friends has me reminding myself this isn't real.

The truth is, there's only been one woman since I've stepped into the Hollywood spotlight that has gotten that honest of a response out of both Bea and Eliza. Gemma Williams and I dated on and off for three years, and to this day, I can't say a single bad thing about her. She was one of the best things to ever happen to me. She couldn't—and shouldn't have had to—deal with the way people talked about her. People I've never met in my life, people who felt they had the right to dictate what was best for me and who I should or shouldn't be with, berated her on social media constantly. She was hated just for being loved by me.

The final straw was when her address was leaked online, and some asshole threw an egg at her. She called moments later to say she couldn't do it anymore. Right then, we both said some pretty awful things to each other. She was scared. I was angry I was losing her over something I had no control over. We've apologized to each other since then, but that changed nothing for her. At least not when it came to me. Last I heard, she was married with a kid or two. Eliza still talks to her every now and then, and even though it's been two years, it still stings.

Not because I miss her or anything like that. I've moved on in that aspect. I just hate the *why* of it. But it's also prepared me. Especially for tonight.

I already spoke to the head of my security about adding someone to the team for Birdie. I don't think she would say anything to me if there was someone harassing her. This will keep her safe and give me peace of mind. I just need to find the right time to tell her.

Birdie sighs in awe when she's back on my arm. "This is like something out of a Jane Austen novel."

"I think that might be my favorite feedback I've gotten all night." Eliza grins before excusing herself to talk to the caterers.

Aunt Bea shakes her head. "She's supposed to be enjoying herself."

"Eliza won't stop until she knows everything is perfect." I shrug, my eyes widening with recognition when the trumpeter announces Zoe and Isaac.

My aunt must recognize their names too, because she gives my arm a gentle squeeze and tells us to have fun before making her way over to a table with a few other school staff members.

To the side of us, the Boston Symphony Orchestra is playing a classical cover of "Don't Stop Believin'" by Journey. Right behind Zoe and Isaac, Nova and Bishop enter the garden, and Birdie's stiffness lessens just slightly.

The typically quiet Margot gasps in disdain. "There is no way they're playing Journey and the dance floor is empty!"

I'm fairly certain this is the first time I've heard her speak, come to think of it.

"Amateurs." Nova rolls her eyes as she pulls me into a hug.

"Someone's gotta be the first out there." I wave them on. "Might as well be you ladies."

"We'll meet you with drinks," Isaac adds, even though his wife is already halfway to the dance floor with the other women.

The three of us head to the bar, waiting our turn for the bartender's attention. Everything came together so fast that I hadn't gotten the chance to talk to Isaac and Bishop about what was happening between me and Birdie.

I'm not sure why, but keeping their respect means a lot to me. I was lying not only to some of the people I loved the most—my aunt and childhood friends—but also people that play a significant role in my career, like my publicist and my agent. As far as they're considered, this relationship Birdie and I have is real.

I can't bring myself to lie to Bishop and Isaac, though. I have a feeling that even if I could, their wives would tell them the truth anyway. Either way, it just seems better coming directly from me.

But every time I try to tell them, someone comes up to say hi or pulls me in for a picture.

"So, you and Birdie?" Bishop nudges me when there's a break in conversation.

"Yeah. But you know, right? That it's just—"

Isaac interjects. "I still feel like we need to give you the 'you hurt her, we hurt you' speech. Birdie is like our baby sister."

"Well, I have no intention of hurting her," I assure them.

I would be lying if I said I wasn't feeling the pressure and intimidation. Not so much from Isaac. Sizing him up, I decide I could take him. Bishop, however, looks like a Viking. And though his arms are hidden underneath his suit jacket, I've seen him in a short-sleeve polo on the golf course. There's no doubt in my mind he could pick me up and throw me across the room if he wanted to.

"Besides, it's not us you have to worry about." Bishop nods his head to the group of *Suffra-Jette* women, still standing in the spot we left them, huddled around Birdie. "It's them."

The bartender hands our beers to us and sends one of the servers to follow us with blackberry lilac lemonades for the girls.

No sooner than they have their drinks in hand, the music shifts into another pop cover.

Over the next few songs, the dance floor begins to fill with more people taking their lead. No matter where she is or who comes up to talk to me, I make sure to keep my eyes on Birdie. Her eyes light up with joy as Campbell twirls her, and she catches me watching midspin.

The pink fabric of her dress seems to float around her. I'm thankful Eliza had the time last night to help me choose dresses for the five women I invited last minute. I wouldn't have pulled it off without Isaac's help, either. He's the one that gave me all their addresses. Admittedly, after the dresses were picked and I had everyone's address, my assistant took care of everything else.

I was worried someone would be upset with their personal information being given out without their consent, but he assured me he would take the blame if necessary. Luckily for all of us, no one has to take any kind of blame, and all the women seem to be over the moon with the dress and shoe choices, and getting to be here tonight.

For the first time since we arrived, a slower tempo song begins to play. With it, the dance floor opens slightly. Taking the musical cue, we three guys join our dates.

"I appreciate the sentiment," Birdie begins, her voice timid and soft as I lead us to a spot to claim as our own, "but you don't have to dance with me."

"Isn't that what people do at balls?" I answer, brushing her off. "Besides, I *want* to dance with you."

She doesn't say anything else as we begin to sway back and forth to the melody. I don't recognize the song playing, but it's quickly becoming one of my favorites.

"Do we have a song?" I muse. "I mean, couples have songs, right? Do we?"

"We probably should. But not this one. This doesn't feel like us."

Strangely enough, I agree. The song is beautiful, and so is the moment it allows us to share together, but there's nothing connecting it to us.

Two additional slow songs play, allowing Birdie and I to fall into rhythm together. It's as if she belongs right here in my arms.

So naturally, a faster song plays next, bursting the little bubble we've managed to stay safely within for the last ten minutes. I can't seem to shake the disappointment when she asks if we should get another drink.

"Is it silly that I'm just soaking up this night? I know this"— she points between the two of us —"is just business, but being here is like something out of a book. Back when people courted. Before swiping left or right and late-night texts. When love was this grand spectacle…"

There it is. There's the opening I need.

"Challenge accepted."

BIRDIE 17.

"CHALLENGE?" I repeat. "What challenge?"

Atticus's lip curls. "To show you that real romance, chivalry, and all that, isn't dead. We have to do this anyway, right? Let me plan the dates. Let me court you."

"You really *have* watched too many rom-coms." I refer back to the conversation with Campbell in the trailer yesterday.

"Oh, come on," he coaxes. When his eyes return to me, he stills for a moment and then lets out a breath. With the slightest tilt of his head, he narrows his eyes as he tries to decipher my silence. But just seconds later, his shoulders relax. "Someone hurt you."

It's not a question, so I don't answer.

But he's right. I wouldn't exactly say I'm a woman scorned, but the only love in the cards for me is the fictional kind I create for Jette.

I've discovered that while men say they want a strong, independent woman, what they *really* mean is they want a strong, independent woman... if she doesn't make more money or isn't more advanced in her career. I refuse to settle or dim my light for anyone.

"Also, I've been thinking," he begins. "I know the plan was for you to just ride home with Campbell and the girls, but if paparazzi are lingering outside and see us leaving separately, someone is going to report that. What would you say if I asked you to sleep in the guest room at my house tonight?"

Again, he's right. All it takes is the wrong person to see us going in two different cars to throw speculation out there. Damn it. I didn't think this would be easy, but I certainly wasn't expecting to have to assume we were being watched all the time...

I also didn't expect to seriously contemplate spending the night at Atticus's house, because I want to see if he looks as handsome first thing in the morning as he does now. Maybe he turns into some hideous swamp monster in the middle of the night.

Atticus Cohen is not Shrek, Birdie. He lives in a million-dollar home in historical Concord, Massachusetts. He smells like a magical forest and looks like hot sex personified.

"Okay, fine," I concede. "But I don't have any clothes."

"I'll take care of it," he says, as if it's as simple as stating that the sky is blue and the grass is green.

"You've been doing that a lot lately." I shake my head. "One of these days, I'm going to have to—"

Our conversation is stopped short when a beautiful brunette approaches us. It only takes me a millisecond to recognize Julia Blackburn. Julia played Atticus's mom in *Sunset Heights*, so it doesn't surprise me she's here. The actor that played his brother and a few of his former castmates have spoken to Atticus throughout the night.

As a fan of the show, it warms my heart to see they're all really as close as they claim they are in interviews. I'm sure every single one of them thinks I'm just the quiet artistic type, as I keep my part in any conversations brief. The truth is, every time one of them walked over to us, whether it was just the two of us or we were with my friends, I was internally losing my shit.

It's been like this all night. I didn't think anyone knew who I was, but I've been asked to take photos with and without Atticus. People I never would have dreamed of meeting in this lifetime have come up to me and told me how much they love my comic book and cannot wait to see it on the big screen.

At one point, I'm quite sure I blacked out and promised Ryan Reynolds I would "personally make sure" he received an invitation to the movie premiere. In hindsight, I don't have the authority to be dishing out promises like that. But who the fuck says no to Deadpool?

"I've been trying to get the nerve to come up to you all night!" I assumed she had come over to talk to Atticus, but she's looking directly at me.

"Me?" I ask, pointing to myself. There's no way in hell *the* Julia Blackburn knows who I am. "I'm sorry. Are you talking to me? You must have me confused with someone else. I'm just—"

"Birdie Yamamoto, right?" She glances over to Atticus wearily. "If not, your girlfriend has an identical twin."

"Oh no. I'm Birdie," I assure her before admitting, "I just didn't think you'd have any clue who I am."

"Are you kidding? *Suffra-Jette* is a huge deal in the Blackburn house," she gushes. "Sunny, my daughter, *loves* your comic. I sent a text to Atticus when I heard the rumors. I just had to tell him how excited Sunny was."

Atticus confirms with a head nod. "She did."

"Anyway," she continues, "I know you're a busy bee, floating around on the man of the hour's arm, but you're such a rock star to her. Would you mind taking a photo with me so I can show her tomorrow? She's only eleven, so she's still too little for events like this." She leans in and lowers her voice before finishing with, "And I think you are the only one she would care about anyway."

As Julia hands Atticus her phone, I stand there, frozen in place, too awestruck by our interaction to move. God, I hope I don't look like a deer in headlights.

"You know, I would be more than happy to send some signed comic books to Sunny. I also have some cool merch just sitting in my office," I tell her when Atticus hands her phone back. "And the rest of the *Suffra-Jette* team is here too. Just over there." I point to where my friends are standing. "If you really want to blow Sunny's mind, I know they would all take a photo."

"Would they really?" Her surprised tone matches how I'm feeling. It's baffling to see someone so excited about meeting me and my friends, especially considering Atticus is standing right at my side. "At the risk of being too pushy, would you be around next week? I'm in between projects right now, and I'm home for a bit. Sunny and I would love to take you out for lunch."

I tell her that I would love to while we walk together. I introduce her to my friends. Though at this point, I'm once again fairly certain I'm in a dream.

At any given moment, I'm going to wake up in my bed. Maybe this is some Wizard of Oz trickery. That's it! This is my Dorothy Gale moment.

After we take photos on Julia's and Campbell's phones— because leave it to Campbell Porter to see a potential opportunity to trend on social media—Atticus returns to my side. His hand settles on the small of my back, and it's equal parts reassuring and terrifying.

The reassurance comes from knowing he's here and, as he promised, we've got this. The fear comes from knowing how fast his very presence has given me assurance.

Francie is chatting Julia's ear off a few feet away, so I take the opportunity to turn to Atticus. "I need you to shake me, pinch me, *something*. I'm pretty sure Julia Blackburn just invited me to lunch. Either I'm dreaming or we're in some alternate universe right now."

I was having a hard enough time wrapping my head around the fact that I've been in the same room as Leonardo DiCaprio all night, but Julia Blackburn just invited me to lunch. There's no way this is my life.

"I think *someone* has watched *Spider-Man: Into the Spider-Verse* too many times," he teases.

"Oh, okay, Mr. Walking Talking Rom-Com. I see what you did there. Way to throw my own shit-talking back in my face."

"What do you say we get out of here?" he asks. "I have to say bye to my sister and my aunt, but I'm ready whenever you are."

"Atticus and I are going to head out," I say loudly, glancing between my friends.

After everyone has been hugged and promised every little detail of Atticus and my "slumber party," he and I begin to make our way over to Bea and Eliza. Another round of hugs and a promise to get together for lunch is made before we try to sneak out a side exit. In the background, "Bad Romance" by Lady Gaga plays, and I lean into him.

"*This.* This is it. This is our song."

ATTICUS 18.

TRYING TO BE A GENTLEMAN, I step back, letting Birdie into the house before me.

Now, if I had thought it through, I would have realized that the worst guard dog in the history of all dogs would be overjoyed to have someone new to play with. Just seconds after Birdie steps over the threshold, Parker makes his grand entrance by barreling down the stairs and running right to her, then circling her at a hundred miles per hour, tail wagging just as fast.

I open my mouth to tell Parker to sit, but I close it just as fast when Birdie bends down and pets him.

"Hi, Parker." She tips her head back in laughter when he peppers her face with slobbery puppy kisses. "I'm Birdie. It's so nice to meet you."

"Alright, alright." I shake my head. "That's enough, Parker."

"There is no such thing as enough puppy kisses," Birdie argues as she stands back up. "He's beautiful, Atticus. No wonder you rescued him."

I look down and give him a rub behind his ears. "He'd been at the shelter for six months when I went there. No one wanted to adopt him because he needed to be in a quiet house with no kids. He was surrendered to the shelter by a wife leaving her abusive husband. Her husband used to kick Parker, so understandably, he was skittish around new people, loud sounds, sudden motions…"

"So you saved him." Her voice is filled with such reverence as she locks eyes with me.

"If I knew that Parker's backstory would be all it took to win you over, I would have told it to you at the table read." I chuckle, nodding toward the kitchen. "Want a snack?" I ask her and at the mention of the s word, Parker barks in acknowledgment. "Yeah, you too, knucklehead."

"Sure," she agrees, following me into the kitchen.

After I grab a few treats for Parker, I head to my favorite drawer in the whole kitchen.

"Take your pick," I tell her, looking down.

Most of the time, but especially now when I'm playing a role in a superhero movie, I eat healthy. However, when I'm in between jobs or really need a little sugar boost, I head to the snack drawer. It's filled with all kinds of nostalgic treats from my childhood.

"You have Dunkaroos?" she exclaims. "These were my favorite as a kid. My mom would never buy them, but Campbell's mom did. I didn't know they still made them."

After Birdie takes a package of Dunkaroos, I sift through until I settle on Gushers *and* Fruit by the Foot.

"There's a drawer like this in my trailer on set too," I say as we each take a seat at the table.

"Looks like I know where I'll be hanging out on set," she says, dipping the little graham cracker cookie into the frosting. "Also, um, I don't remember in the midst of all of tonight's craziness if I've gotten the chance to say thank you."

"There's no need." I brush off her thank-you, tearing open the package of Gushers. "The gala is always fun, but I forgot it was work for a bit tonight. That's never happened. And the only thing different this year is that you and the *Suffra-Jette* team were there. I had a fun time."

"I did too," she agrees. "But that doesn't change the fact that you went above and beyond for not only me but my friends too."

"Dance with me," I say, offering her my hand. "One last dance. Just you and me. What do you say?"

"But there's no music." She shakes her head.

"I can change that in two seconds," I rebut, glancing over to the speaker on the counter. "If I put on music, will you dance with me?"

"Okay, fine. But you can't pick the song." She smirks. "Whatever song plays first, that's what you get. That's what we dance to."

To say I have eclectic taste in music would be putting it mildly. My music library has everything from Tupac to Nirvana to Taylor Swift. There are even songs from the *Frozen* soundtrack from my niece's Elsa phase. This could either be a complete bust or an epic finale to an already perfect night.

"Alexa," I call out. "Play my music."

"(Everything I do) I Do It for You" by Bryan Adams begins to play, and I pull my lip in. I couldn't have picked a better, cheesier love song if I tried. And because I'm no amateur, I know it's the full version of the song. All six minutes and thirty-something seconds of it.

"Tell me something I should know," I say quietly, hoping the intimacy of the moment we're sharing will allow Birdie to tell me something real.

"I was wrong about you," she whispers. "Tell me something I should know."

"I was right about you."

When we were still at the gala, Birdie said tonight felt like a dream, and I finally understand.

"You were wrong earlier, though," I whisper as the instrumental bridge begins. "*This* is our song."

Birdie

STAYING HERE TONIGHT IS A BAD IDEA.

Dancing with Atticus is an even worse idea.

But believing I can come out of this ordeal without catching feelings is the worst one of all.

There isn't a single moment in Atticus's arms when I'm not hoping he'll kiss me. And then again when he has me follow him to his bedroom to get a T-shirt and a pair of sweatpants. And when he shows me the guest bedroom.

He doesn't, though. He's a complete gentleman. Because of course he is.

So now I lie in his bed. Well, not *his* bed, but a bed in his house, wishing I had enough nerve to do something about the fact that I want to march back across the hall and just kiss his stupidly perfect lips.

I could always use the fake-relationship card. There will be a point we'll have to kiss in front of other people. We should practice, right?

But what if I'm reading everything wrong and this is one-sided? What if he's just acting the part? The "romance is real" challenge he came up with at the gala seems far beyond what we're trying to accomplish here. And *he's* the one that asked me to dance in the kitchen.

It's been a while since I've second-guessed myself when it comes to a man. For a long time now, my only relationship, if you could even call it that, has been late-night hookups with the man Campbell refers to as "Tinder Guy." My other friends don't know about him. It's just sex. And even that stopped six months ago.

Part of me wishes I still hated Atticus. Hate was so much easier than this. At least then I was certain in my feelings. There was no gray area in despising him.

What was Campbell thinking putting the two of us together like this? This is a bad idea. This is an unbelievably bad idea.

I'M unhappy to report that after a full night of sleep, waking up, drinking coffee, and riding back to my house next to Atticus, I still want to kiss him. He dropped me off around nine, just to go home and come back a few hours later for family dinner at my parents' house.

I'm putting the final additions on my makeup when the doorbell rings.

"I got it!" Campbell yells as I close my tube of mascara. I slide on a pair of canvas shoes and grab my bag. By the time I get down the hallway, Campbell and Atticus are heading up the stairs.

"God, Atticus. Do you ever not look perfect?" Campbell scoffs playfully. "Please tell me he looks rough when he wakes up. There's gotta be some catch."

When I see him, I have to agree with my best friend. Sporting a solid black long-sleeve T-shirt and slim, tapered jeans, his outfit is simple yet somehow still so goddamn sexy. His hair is tucked into a navy Red Sox hat. I already know that's going to score him some points with my dad.

"Sorry to disappoint." I shrug. "But bedhead and gray sweatpants—"

"Stop it right there!" Her eyes widen. "Did you say *gray sweatpants*? I know you two are only fake dating, but how did you not for real jump his bones?"

"You know I'm standing right here." Atticus raises his brows, but the overconfident smirk on his lips gives him away. "And who says 'jump his bones' anymore?"

"Oh, I'm sorry, Hollywood," Campbell apologizes before she turns to me. "How did you not jump on his cock and fuck him crazy?" Facing Atticus, she challenges him with raised brows of her own. "Better?"

"Campbell!" I gasp, glancing over to Atticus.

But if he's even the tiniest bit embarrassed, he certainly doesn't show it.

"Shall we?" he asks, looking down at his watch. "I don't want to show up late and give your dad anymore reason to not like me."

"You two go ahead." Campbell waves. "I have a few emails I need to send out before I head over there. I'll be right behind you."

As soon as we step outside, warm spring sunlight touches my skin, and a unique happiness that only sunshine can bring fills my body.

Everyone loves autumn in New England. Don't get me wrong, I appreciate a good pumpkin spice latte and wear my Uggs as much as the next girl, but there's something to be said about springtime. The sound of birds happily tweeting after the frigid winter. The pop of bright green in the trees. January may start the new year, but spring always feels like a new beginning to me.

I've written my favorite comics in the springtime. Easter is my favorite holiday. My favorite little woodland friends always return in the spring too.

My therapist says that sunshine releases endorphins like serotonin, and I mean, technically, she's right. But really, I just like seeing all the pretty budding flowers. The stuffiness of winter leaves when we can start opening windows and let fresh air into the house again. The energy is different in spring.

"Should we drive over there together?" Atticus asks when I stop in front of the driver's side of my car and fish for my keys. "I just assumed, but—"

"Probably," I say, pulling my hand from the bag. "Your car or mine?"

"I'll drive," he offers, walking to the passenger side of his car. After opening it for me, he waits until I'm settled in the seat to close the door. Once he's in his own seat, he starts the car and turns to me. "How about some hype music? I feel like I need it."

Before "This Is War" is done playing, we pull into my parents' driveway. There's only one other car there. Since Campbell is still at our house and her parents just have to walk across the street, I assume it's the new car Cash talked about at the *Suffra-Jette* signing.

Atticus sighs, looking up to the house. "So, yep. Meeting your dad is just as scary this time as it was two weeks ago."

"You were scared to meet my dad?" I question. "Could have fooled me."

"Oh yeah," Atticus confirms, stepping out of the car. He opens the door behind him and pulls out a bouquet of my mom's favorite flowers and a bottle of my dad's whiskey.

To quote Francie: "We stan a man who does his research."

"You'll be fine," I promise him. "If all else fails, talk about the Red Sox. They're Dad's favorite team too."

"I see that Google search is serving you well." Atticus chuckles as we walk right into my childhood home.

Following the voices, we find my parents and Cash in the kitchen. Mom looks up at the sound of our footsteps, her eyes lighting up at the sight of us.

"Birdie, Atticus!" She beams. "Hi. I'm so glad you could make it. I know you both must be so busy, being the new Hollywood "It" couple!"

"Mom." I roll my eyes. "Please be chill."

"Oh, I'm chill. It was *People* magazine that said it first." She grins, realizing Atticus is holding a bouquet of daisies. "Are those for me?"

"They are," he says, handing them to her. Turning to my dad, he hands him the bottle of Kaiyo Mizunara Oak Whisky. "And this is for you."

"What can I do to help?" I ask my mom.

"Can you run downstairs and get a bottle of red and a bottle of white?" she asks. "Something that will pair well with salmon and roasted vegetables."

My head tilts in confusion at her request. I want to help, but does she remember to whom she's talking? I drink ten-dollar wine from a box.

"I'll help," Cash offers and my stomach drops. He hasn't so much as looked in my direction since Atticus and I walked into the room.

"Perfect. Thank you!" Mom doesn't give either of us another glance before turning to Atticus. "Birdie tells us you're a Sox fan! We love us some Red Sox in this house. Don't we, Ken?"

I never told her that, but I'm grateful for her stepping in and creating a bridge between Dad and Atticus. No matter the truth of what's happening between me and Atticus, it obviously means a lot to him to get my parents' approval. After needing to make sure Atticus's aunt and sister liked me last night, I get it.

What I *don't* get is wine. I also don't get why Cash needs to be down here with me. Well, no, that's a lie. I do get it. I'm just not ready for the conversation that's about to take place.

Cash has known me just as long as Campbell has. Lying to him feels wrong, but it's not just that.

"So does he know?" Cash asks as soon as we get to the wall of wine. "Does your boyfriend know about us?"

"No one knows about us, Cash." I roll my eyes. "That's the way you wanted it, remember?"

It's been six months since I answered one of his late-night texts.

Cash, the artist formerly known as "Tinder Guy."

At least because that's the lie I told Campbell when she would ask who I was sneaking off to meet up with late at night. "He's no one. Just some guy I met on Tinder. It's just sex. Nothing more."

Well, it wasn't entirely a lie. It was just sex. And our agreement was that the second one of us starts dating someone seriously, it all stops. No questions asked. Cash and I were a matter of convenience.

Though, it hasn't always been like that. At least not for me.

Cash Porter was my first love. My first everything, really. And no one knows. Not even Campbell. *Especially* not Campbell.

It doesn't matter that Cash was the one that kissed me when we were fourteen. It doesn't matter that it was *his* hand that crept up *my* skirt in the woods behind their summer cabin two years later. Cash is Campbell's brother. I'm her best friend. And that is a line you don't cross without expecting some serious repercussions.

I am right in the middle of the two of them age wise. Campbell is a year older than me; Cash is a year younger than me. So when she left for college, sneaking around became much easier.

All it took was me saying that I was going across the street to work on homework with Cash. My parents never thought anything of it.

Halfway through my senior year of high school, he started dating someone in his grade. He didn't even tell me. I walked in on them kissing one afternoon. I didn't think anything of it when I let myself into his house. I'd been doing it longer than I could remember.

Part of me always thought he did it on purpose because he

was too much of a coward to tell me. The other part knew it was because what we had was never anything more than sex to him. I was just the girl next door. His sister's nerdy friend. I wasn't the girl he would walk around school with. I would never be his girlfriend.

Cash was my first lesson in detachment. When he finally acknowledged what happened, I brushed him off, and that changed everything for us. I stopped going over, and when I had to, I always knocked first. When my mom asked me about it, I just blamed his new relationship. Which wasn't a lie, but not exactly the entire truth either.

Moving to Boston for college was the best thing that could have happened for me that summer. There wasn't time to be sad or think of Cash. That is, until a year later when he strolled into the toga party my sorority was hosting. Too many drinks for both of us turned into a drunken bathroom hookup, which turned into a drunken bedroom hookup, which led to breakfast the next morning and plans to meet at another party later.

I'm not naïve enough to think I was the only girl Cash was fucking, and he certainly wasn't the only guy I was sleeping with... until we both moved back home. Cash moved to Townsend first. He accepted a job at our former high school as a gym teacher right out of college.

I followed suit about a year later when I was offered a job as a staff writer for Coolidge Comics. Unlike my former place of employment, which required writers to come into the building every day, Isaac and Zoe believe writers and artists should have the freedom to create wherever they choose. We have both the comic shop and the office space to utilize if we want to. Campbell goes up twice a week if the weather is good. Ramona, Francie, and Margot all live in town, so they're in the office space a lot. But I only go up when I must for meetings or to drop something off for Zoe.

The night I moved into my townhome, Cash brought over

avocado rolls and the first box of wine to go into my fridge. I still don't know how he knew where to find me. Probably my mom.

Our new-house celebratory dinner turned into new-house celebratory sex, and then we kept finding reasons to hookup. Wedding sex. Finished-before-my-deadline sex. Just-because-it's-Tuesday sex. But then I just decided I was done.

I stopped answering his texts. They were the same every time. Never before ten o'clock at night and always began with "Hey, what are you up to?" If he had just texted me once during the daytime, I might have reconsidered, but he didn't. And eventually, he stopped texting altogether.

"Does he fuck you like I do?" Cash whispers, brushing my chest with his arm as he reaches for a bottle of wine on the other side of me. "Can Mr. Hollywood make you tremble like I can?"

My skin grows hot with anger. He doesn't want me. Not really. If he did, he would have done something other than send the occasional text at two in the morning trying to get some ass. He just wants what he thinks another man has. And if he doesn't think I can see that, he's a fucking idiot.

"Fuck off, Cash."

I grab the first bottle of red and then white that I see, not giving any regard to if it will pair well with lunch, and head up the stairs. Leaving the wine on the kitchen counter, I pull Atticus away from a conversation with my dad.

"Sorry, Dad. I just need to borrow Atticus for a second," I tell him.

I don't wait for a response before leading Atticus out of the sliding door that goes to the deck. As soon as we're behind the safety of the closed door, I tell him the decade-long secret. The words spill out of me faster than I can stop them. I don't know why I feel like I owe him the truth. I just knew as soon as I walked away from Cash, Atticus needed to know.

"When we were downstairs looking for the wine, he asked me

if you fucked me like he did." My stomach tightens and my cheeks flush with embarrassment.

"What did you say?" Atticus asks, his brows quirking in interest.

It's the first thing he's said since I started spilling my guts to him.

"I told him to fuck off." I shrug. "In hindsight, I *should* have told him you were better."

"He's been watching us the whole time we've been out here. I can feel it," Atticus says. With one hand, he pulls me to him. His hold is tighter than it was last night. It's possessive. "He knows you're telling me."

On instinct, I look back through the door, and sure enough, Cash is standing with arms crossed, watching the two of us with a scowl.

Atticus cups my chin with his hand, pulling my attention back to him. As soon as we're facing each other, he gently tips my head up.

"If you were my girlfriend, I would want him to know you were mine," he whispers, sending a trail of goose bumps up my arms and down my spine. "And that I *definitely* fuck you better."

ATTICUS 20.

FAKE RELATIONSHIP OR NOT, after everything Birdie just said, there is no way in hell I'm going to sit back and let a fuckboy like Cash Porter think I'm anything less than obsessed with her. This is me selfishly using my ugly duckling past against him. Growing up, I was not the dude that got chicks. I had a bowl cut, I was in theater, and I had no game. Guys like Cash threw guys like me into lockers.

There's also the fact that I've spent approximately two and a half days being Birdie's fake boyfriend, and I already know she's too good to be someone's decade-long booty call. I also knew as soon as I realized Cash was watching us that I had to kiss her. Like, *really* kiss her.

When my lips pressed against hers, I didn't expect my heart to race. I didn't expect her body to melt into mine, or the way her hands gripped my shirt like she needed to steady herself. Traces of peppermint and vanilla on her soft, plush lips pulled me under, and the kiss became something I wanted, something I needed. It was no longer about proving something to Cash or anyone else.

As much as I don't want to, I pull back just enough to break the kiss.

If I don't do it now, I'm going to find my way back to her lips.

"We should go back in there," I whisper.

"Do we have to?" She sighs. "I think I'd rather stay out here."

"Don't tempt me," I tell her, wishing that we could.

I step away slightly, pulling her hand, which is still balled up in my shirt, and sliding it into my own.

"What were you and my dad talking about?" she asks, her other hand on the door handle.

"You," I answer honestly. "And catching a Sox game after filming wraps."

While we were out on the deck, Campbell, my aunt, and two people I presume are Cash and Campbell's parents joined everyone else in the kitchen.

Despite being told not to bring something, my aunt also showed up with a bouquet of flowers and a tin undoubtedly filled with her infamous chocolate truffles.

"Something to keep in the back of your mind." Birdie's mom nudges me with her elbow after thanking my aunt for the flowers. "Daffodils are my daughter's favorite flowers."

"Noted. Thank you." I smile as I greet Campbell. "Hey, bestie."

"Oh, hey, bestie." She laughs as I reference a *very* drunk, *very* friendly Campbell last night. We get a slew of funny looks pointed in our direction, so she explains, "After quite a few boozy lemonades, I decided since I'm Birdie's best friend, Atticus and I are besties now too."

Out of my peripheral vision, I see Birdie in Aunt Bea's arms, and I would be lying if I said it didn't make my heart swell twice in size.

I don't think there's any sense in denying that real emotions are infiltrating this pretend relationship. There's just something about seeing Birdie embracing the woman that raised me that fills me with joy. I can't be a mama's boy because I don't have a mom, but if an auntie's boy is a thing, that's me. I would give Aunt Bea the world if she would let me. She won't take anything from me unless I manage to somehow masquerade it as a gift.

"That's your money, Atticus," she always says. "One day you will have a wife and babies to spoil. Save your pennies for them."

There's nothing anyone can say or do that will convince me Beatrice Cohen isn't an angel walking on earth.

My aunt asks Birdie if she had fun last night, and I take the moment to introduce myself to Campbell's parents.

There's no mistaking the family resemblance between the Porter women. Both have the same raven hair, fair skin, and silver-blue eyes.

"And you must be Campbell's older sister." When I offer the elder Campbell woman my hand, she narrows her eyes and smirks at my flattery.

"And you are just as charming as my daughter says you are, Atticus," she says, taking my hand. "I'm Bridget, and this is my husband, Ron."

"There is no way either of you are old enough to have adult children." I feign disbelief. When Bridget lets go of my hand, I immediately extend it to Ron.

"Atticus Cohen," I tell him, matching his firm grip with my own.

Much like Ken had earlier in the week, he looks me up and down, no doubt assessing me to see if I'm good enough for Birdie.

It's petty as fuck, I'm fully aware, but I'm going to have every one of the people that Cash loves eating out of the palm of my hand by the time we leave here today. Even Campbell. This isn't territorial jealousy. I know Birdie's not mine. But fuck him for making her ever feel like she wasn't good enough for anything more than a secret hookup.

"Can we please talk about those dresses you two were

wearing last night?" Bridget looks back and forth between Birdie and Campbell. "I felt like I was on memory lane, looking at your prom photos."

"Weren't they gorgeous?" Campbell gushes before turning to me. "I never got the chance to say thank you for making sure we all got the princess treatment." Facing her parents, she continues, "Atticus not only sent dresses and shoes for all us girls but he also arranged for a whole glam squad to do our hair and makeup before the gala."

Campbell Porter is the best damn hype woman ever.

Birdie

AFTER DINNER, WE HEAD OUTSIDE WHEN MY FATHER makes the comment that it's too nice to spend the rest of the night in the house.

"So, Atticus," Cash starts before taking a swig of his beer. "This thing with you and Birdie happened quickly, don't you think? I mean, you've known her for all of, what, two minutes?"

"Cash!" his mother gasps out. "Don't be rude."

"It's fine." Atticus's smile is small as he reassures her and seamlessly closes the space between us, his hand sliding into the back pocket of my jeans. "Sometimes you just know, ya know? I wasn't about to sit back and wait for another guy to come in and steal her attention when I wanted it all for myself."

After he presses a kiss on the top of my head, I look up to him. I pull my top lip in to hide the smirk growing on my lips. I know he used those words specifically after being given the information about Cash and me. And from the way Cash flexes his hand, slowly balling it into a fist before letting it go, so does he.

Shoulda, woulda, coulda, buddy.

"It surprised me when I first heard too," Atticus's aunt says from the patio couch she's sharing with my mom. "But it only takes a few minutes being around these two to get it. They stole the show last night."

"I wouldn't go that far." I blush, knowing damn well it was Atticus who stole the show. I spent most of the night dancing with my friends and quietly clinging to his arm because I had such anxiety about making an ass out of myself.

"Did Birdie tell you that Julia Blackburn wants to take her out to lunch?" Atticus asks no one in particular. "Julia's daughter is a *Suffra-Jette* fan, and Julia all but fangirled meeting Birdie last night."

"She did not fangirl." I brush off Atticus's praise. It wasn't a direct compliment, but it still makes me feel like I want to crawl out of my skin. I don't know why I'm like this. Compliments, presents, being the center of attention—none of that is my jam.

"I would," Campbell argues. "That reminds me. I should post the photo of us with her. Hopefully, I don't look how I felt."

Atticus's aunt chuckles. "Those lemonades were really good. I bet we can figure out how to make them."

"Ohhh! We can have them at the next family dinner," Mom offers. "You two will be coming next month, right?"

"If the invitation is open, I'll be here." Bea grins.

The guilt settles in my stomach again as I watch a new friendship growing. My mom is the kindest person I've ever known, and Bea Cohen is a kindred spirit if I've ever seen one.

"Eliza should come next month!" Campbell exclaims. I mean, maybe I've lost my mind here, but as the one person who knows Atticus and I aren't a real couple, why in the hell is she suggesting we all get together like one big happy family?

Because this is what she wants.

The only problem is, I think I might want it too.

ATTICUS 21.

OVER THE NEXT FIVE DAYS, the only time Birdie and I see each other is on set. I'm on the call sheet every day. Having her here has made me step up my game, that's for damn sure. If I thought I was giving one hundred percent before, I was wrong. I just want to make her proud.

While I wait to be called to set, we spend time together in my trailer. Hair and makeup know her by name because she showed up on Monday with a catered order of bagels, muffins, juices, and coffee. Most mornings, she leaves the trailer with her hair done too, though she never asks for it.

Sometimes someone else pops in, but for the most part, it's just the two of us.

Neither of us has mentioned the kiss at her parents' house, but I've thought about it approximately fifty-two billion times.

Sometimes we run lines. She laughs every time I tell her that she may have missed her calling as an actress.

"You should ask Haley for a walk-on role," I tell her after we've gone through today's lines.

"Don't you worry. I have my Stan Lee moment," she says, referencing comic legend Stan Lee's notorious cameo appearances in Marvel television and film productions.

"You do?" This is news to me. "Why didn't you tell me?"

Her lip curls into a smirk. "It was supposed to be a surprise."

"Are you free tomorrow night or Sunday during the day?" I ask. "I promised Mila I would go to her soccer game tomorrow, but I have an idea for a date night."

"I have plans tomorrow, but I'm free Sunday," Birdie answers. "Why, what's up?"

"I have an idea for a date," I repeat, which causes her to raise her eyebrows in suspicion. "Or did you forget? I'm supposed to be making you believe in real romance, fake girlfriend."

"I didn't forget. I just thought you did," she admits, taking a seat with her mug of tea.

I didn't forget. I've spent the week soaking up every moment I've gotten to spend with Birdie. In the last five days, I've learned she has a competitive streak—especially when it comes to losing video games. She doesn't like coffee but loves a good cup of tea. She loves breakfast food but hates eating in the morning. There's always a notebook and a sketchpad in the canvas tote bag she takes everywhere with her.

"Tell me something I should know," she says before I can tell her that not only did I *not* forget about our date but I also spent all week trying to come up with an idea worthy of her.

"I don't remember my parents," I tell her without giving it much thought. "And the only people I'm jealous of on this earth are my aunt and my sister, because they do."

Once those words have been said, I know there's no going back, and I'm going to have to talk about it now.

I have done my best to keep my private life out of the spotlight. The media has been able to dig up enough information that they can piece together most of what happened, and I always make sure that my family, especially my parents, are listed in the off-limits topics in interviews. It's usually the only thing I ever have listed.

"Oh, Atticus." Birdie clutches her heart. She reaches across the table, then takes my hand in hers.

"I love Aunt Bea," I say. "And I'm so grateful for everything she did and sacrificed for Eliza and me, but I don't know. Some days I'd like to know for myself if I got my dad's laugh like Aunt Bea says. Stuff like that."

Orphaned at just three years old, it's been just me, Eliza, and Aunt Bea for as long as I can remember. My parents dropped us off for a sleepover and never came back. A selfish drunk driver took their lives on their tenth wedding anniversary.

Not only was he intoxicated but he also fled the scene and left them there to die. He had been so inebriated that he didn't realize the entire front bumper of his car fell off as he drove my parents' station wagon into an oak tree. The police found and arrested him before the sun rose the next day.

"Aunt Bea told us there was an accident," I tell her, the comfort of her hand on mine giving me strength to keep talking. "Sometime around my eighth birthday, which coincidentally fell on the same week as my parents' wedding anniversary, I overheard her talking to someone on the phone about it. She thought I was in bed. I never made it to the kitchen. It was right around then that I became obsessed with Peter Parker—and Spider-Man, too."

In the years that followed, much like how Peter Parker sought to avenge his uncle's murder, I imagined finding the man who had taken my parents from me. I never had a plan beyond coming face-to-face with him, but I played it out in my head over and over until it was an unhealthy obsession. Retrospectively, it was a good thing the internet wasn't as easily accessible as it is today. Vengeance was best left as an unattainable idea. A younger version of me wouldn't have hesitated to hop on a Greyhound bus to Daytona, Florida, where Douglas Earl

Simpson IV spent the rest of his days after he finished his prison sentence.

I don't talk about any of it for a lot of reasons—the look of pity in people's eyes for one. But there's no pity in Birdie's eyes when I tell her about how I spiraled around my eighteenth birthday, looking for information on them and Douglas.

"I can't say I understand losing your parents the way you did," she says. "But I do know what it's like to not want to hurt the people you love who selflessly chose to love you. Most days I'm okay not knowing where I came from—I'm Annie and Ken Yamamoto's daughter. But it's not exactly like I claim my dad's Japanese heritage or truly celebrate being Irish on St. Patrick's Day with my mom."

There's a small rap on the door, and someone calls out to let me know they're ready for me on set.

An assistant is waiting for us outside of the trailer in a cart.

"Do you think they're in a rush to get me to set?" I ask the assistant, my hand sliding into Birdie's when we're both on flat ground. Small public displays of affection aren't new to the two of us at this point, but after our conversation in the trailer, it feels intimate. *Real.* "Or do you think we have the time to walk?"

"I think you're Atticus Cohen, and they'll wait if you want them to." The younger man chuckles nervously. He can't be much more than eighteen or nineteen, scoring the job as a benefit of being a crew member's kid.

"I don't want you to give me the answer you think I want to hear." I laugh. "I also don't want you to get into trouble."

"I appreciate that, man." The assistant smiles. "My answer still stands, though."

"Well, in that case, Birdie and I will be there in a few minutes."

Nodding in understanding, he gives us a little wave before pulling off.

"Okay, I have to know." Birdie grins as we walk together

toward Studio B. "Who is your favorite Spider-Man?"

"Comic book Spidey or movie Spidey?" I ask. "Because those answers are very different."

She shrugs. "Both?"

"Well, talking comic books, I have to go with Cosmic Spider-Man. I mean, how can you fuck with the Enigma Force? Who is yours?"

"Okay, one, I'm genuinely impressed right now. Two, I know this is going to be anticlimactic, but Spider-Gwen hands down," she answers. "Aside from Jette, she's my favorite comic book character. One of my most prized comics in my collection is a copy of *Edge of Spider-Verse #2* signed by Jason Latour and Robbi Rodriguez. Gwen Stacy had been part of the comics for a long time as one of Peter Parker's girlfriends, but she didn't become the super-powered version until 2014." Stopping herself, she apologizes. "Sorry. I forget that not everyone loves comics like I do."

"You have nothing to be sorry for. I think being passionate about something is sexy as fuck."

"Movie web slinger?" she asks, her cheeks rosy with embarrassment when I insinuate she's sexy as fuck. I know they exist, but I've never met or been able to talk comic books with a woman before. Given who Birdie is, it's hard to believe we went this long before having a conversation like this. I have a feeling it's the first of many, and I can't wait to hear what else she has to say.

"For a long time, it was Tobey. It's hard to compete with the original." I grin. "But I have to say, I really dig what they did with Spider-Verse, so I'm going to go with your girl's boo, Miles Morales."

"I can respect that," she says as we approach Studio B.

"What about you?" I ask.

"Can I default to Spider-Gwen again? Because, if not, I honestly can't choose," she says. "I loved Andrew and Emma's

chemistry in *The Amazing Spider-Man*. I have an emotional attachment to Tom Holland's story arc and the way he fits into the
Marvel Cinematic Universe. And like you said, it's hard to
compete with the original when it comes to Tobey. Everything
about *Into the Spider-Verse* makes my heart happy."

As we approach where Zoe and Isaac are standing off to the
side, I prepare to say bye to Birdie.

Should I kiss her?

Fuck, I really want to.

"So nice of you to join us, Mr. Cohen," the director teases
when she catches sight of me.

The rumors about her being every actor's dream director is
true. She just wants the best. No matter how many takes actors
need, no matter how many times they screw up their lines or
their blocking, she wants whatever it takes to make the scene as
good as it can get. "Whenever you're ready, you just let us know."

Today we're shooting my fight scenes. It's like choreographing
a dance. Otto has no superpowers. Everything is of his own
doing. So each movement must be perfect to make it believable.
No one will think I've punched a henchman in the face if I don't
perfectly complete the stunt. I could have my stunt double fill in
for moments like this like Violet did in her scenes, but selfishly, I
want to do as much as they'll let me.

Just as I'm about to lean in to leave a kiss on Birdie's forehead, I realize my cell phone is still in my pocket. Pulling it out,
I'm just about to ask Birdie to keep it for me, when I see the
weather alert on my lock screen. My stomach drops when I think
of Parker at home by himself. There isn't much my dog fears, but
if we're talking in superhero terms, thunder is to Parker what
Kryptonite is to Superman.

"I know this is going to sound ridiculous, and I don't mean to
be a pain in the ass," I start. "I just need a few minutes to call
someone to get my dog. I just got an alert about severe thunder-
storms, and he's terrified of them."

BIRDIE 22.

"I CAN GO GET HIM," I offer without hesitation.

That is the girlfriendly thing to do, right? Plus, the thought of Parker being scared breaks my heart a little bit.

"Are you sure?" Atticus asks. "I usually ask my aunt or my sister, but—"

"They left this morning for Mila's cheer competition," I finish. "I know. Eliza was texting me photos of Mila in her uniform. So cute."

His eyebrows pinch in confusion. "We're going to come back to the fact that you and my sister are apparently best friends." His lips curl up in the midst of his worry for Parker. "Are you sure? About grabbing Parker. You can stay at my house and wait it out. Just the thought of him sitting there, alone, scared..."

"If I leave now, I can beat the severe weather," I tell him, looking at the weather app on my phone. It's not supposed to start for a couple of hours. "If you think he'll be okay at my house, I'll take him there. I have some work I can get done and those treats my mom made him that I keep forgetting to bring."

"I still can't believe she made peanut butter treats for him."
Atticus chuckles before exhaling. "Okay. I'll text you the security
code to get into my house. His leash is by the front door. I have a
weighted blanket for him in the office. Sometimes that helps.
He's going to want to curl up with you. Please text me when you
get to my house... and then yours too."

I nod. "You're cute when you're in dad mode."

"It's not just Parker I'm worried about," he says before he
leans down and presses his lips to my forehead.

"We'll be fine," I promise him. "But if I want to beat the
storm, I really need to go."

There isn't a cloud in the sky when I step out of the studio.
That doesn't mean anything in New England, though. Mother
Nature is temperamental. Real talk: she reminds of me when I'm
PMSing.

In one second, I can be fine, and then I'll be crying over the
smallest, tiniest thing. Last month it was because Dairy Queen
didn't have the Blizzard filling I wanted. Ice cream. *I cried over ice
cream.*

But in this case, it's more like a snowstorm in the middle of
May or warm sunshine and seventy-degree temperatures on
Christmas Day—both of which have happened in my lifetime.
Today, it's an early spring storm brought on by a random burst of
heat and humidity.

The setting sun only presses the importance of getting to Atticus's house and then mine sooner rather than later. I want to
make sure Parker is okay, but I definitely do not want to be
driving in the middle of a storm.

Time on set is irrelevant, so I didn't realize until I came out
that it was getting late. Atticus had been waiting all day to be
called, which was fine by me. That meant we got more time to
spend together.

Before I get to the parking lot, Atticus texts me his address and the security code. He also sends me a hundred dollars with the notation that dinner is on him tonight.

I know him well enough by now to know he would be offended if I returned the money to him, and that's the only reason I don't. As promised, I text him to let him know when I arrive. After putting in his security code, I let myself in. Much like the first time I met him, Parker gets a running start to greet me.

"Hi, buddy!" I say, reaching down to pet him. Before I ask him if he wants to go on a ride, I wander down the hallway, peeking into rooms until I find Atticus's office. The last time I was here, it was late, and I only saw the kitchen and the guest room before we left the next morning.

The décor is very Atticus. Nothing too showy. Warm, earthy tones of browns, greens, and whites fill the space.

On a worn brown leather armchair, right where he said it would be, is a gray weighted blanket. A wall-to-wall built-in bookshelf grabs my attention, making me wish we weren't racing the clock to beat this storm. I wish I had the time to browse through his collection. I make a mental note to come back and look through his books the next time I'm here.

Artwork and photos of his nieces take up an entire shelf of their own, and it reminds me of the corkboard I have in my office filled with drawings and notes from Zoe's daughter and Ramona's son.

"Alright, bud," I start, looking down at Parker. He's been at my heels the entire time. Atticus was right about one thing—Parker is the worst guard dog. "Wanna go for a ride to my house?"

As soon as I say "ride," Parker starts zooming around me. "I'll take that as a yes."

Once I manage to get his leash on him, I let him into the back seat of my car, figuring that will give him the most room during our forty-five-minute drive to my house. In hindsight, I should have just taken Atticus up on his offer to stay at his house.

The storm rolls in faster than anticipated. *Much faster.*

Driving a small Volkswagen with a sixty-pound husky trying to sit in my lap while it's torrentially downpouring is a lot harder than I ever imagined it would be. Thankfully, I left his leash attached to his collar, because as soon as I open the car door when we get to my house, Parker all but drags me to the front door.

When I push the door open, I let go of the leash as he runs inside.

I kick off my shoes, leaving them by the door. I walk up the small flight of stairs that leads to the second floor of our town-home. Campbell laughs and points to the kitchen when I get to the top of the landing.

"Are you missing someone?" she asks, pausing the episode of *New Girl* that she's watching. After years of trying to get her to watch it, she finally started it the other day, and it's safe to say she understands my love for Nick Miller now.

"Atticus is working late on stunts," I tell her. "I offered to grab Parker because someone is scared of thunder."

The first crack of lightning lights up the kitchen and incites a howl from Parker. Over the next thirty minutes, I do everything I can think of to coax him out from underneath the kitchen table. There's no other option but to join him. So, with a pillow, his weighted blanket, and my laptop, I crawl under the table with him.

"Hey, fella," I say in the midst of a yawn. "Your dad told me you're a big fan of Spider-Man. So am I."

I open the laptop, go to my files, and find my downloaded copy of *Spider-Man: Into the Spider-Verse.* I hum along with Miles Morales as he sings "Sunflower" by Post Malone. Once he realizes I'm staying put, Parker snuggles into me, and I kiss the top of his head.

"It's okay, buddy," I reassure him. "I got you."

Atticus

IT'S WELL PAST MIDNIGHT WHEN WE WRAP FOR THE night, but I want nothing more than to make sure Birdie and Parker are okay after the storm. We didn't hear too much from inside the studio, but after Campbell sent me a photo of Birdie and Parker sleeping together under their kitchen table, I knew I wasn't heading right home.

> **Me:** *Any chance you'll still be up in about 45 mins? I'm gonna head up that way and save her from the kitchen floor.*
> **Campbell:** *I'll be in bed, but I'll leave the door unlocked. Just lock it behind you.*
> **Me:** *Perfect. Thanks, bestie!*

I put my phone down on the passenger seat, then start the car and begin the drive to New Hampshire. Not even a few miles down the road, "Bad Romance" by Lady Gaga begins to play on the radio. I don't usually believe in signs, but heading to Birdie and hearing the song she dubbed as ours at the gala sure as fuck feels like one.

It doesn't make sense to be feeling like this so soon. We've known each other for just a few weeks at this point. What a whirlwind three weeks it's been. I can't seem to wrap my head around it all. I'm very much a black-and-white person when it comes to relationships. At least I like to think so. I try my damnedest not to string anyone along under false pretenses, even if it's just a hookup.

This entire thing with Birdie is a false pretense, but it feels more real than some of the long-term relationships I've been in. I find myself looking forward to the days I'm on the call sheet because I know I'll see her. And then she does something like this? How am I *not* supposed to be feeling something for her?

As Campbell said, the front door is unlocked. The small staircase of their split-entry condominium leads right to their living room, which opens to their eat-in kitchen. During the day, it's naturally bright due to the picture window in the living room, but right now, the late-night darkness covers the space like a blanket.

Two wooden chairs that have been pushed neatly into the table every time I've been here are in the middle of the kitchen floor, allowing me to bend down and see my big baby of a sixty-pound husky curled up against Birdie on the hard tile floor. The gray weighted blanket I had her grab covers them both, and her laptop lies open in front of them.

And all I can think is that if she's this wonderful with my dog, she's going to make an amazing mother one day.

Shaking it off as a delirious, overtired thought, I whisper Parker's name and gently rub Birdie's side.

"I'll just take him out for a quick walk, and then we'll be out of your hair." I stifle a yawn. "I owe you big time, Birdie."

"You don't owe me anything," she says, taking my hand as she slowly stands up. She glances over to the clock on the stove and shakes her head. "It's one in the morning. You can just crash here for the night."

Attaching Parker's leash to his collar, I tell her we'll be right back. Parker goes to the bathroom as soon as his paws touch the grass. When he's done, he walks right back up the steps to the front door. Even my dog can't wait to get back to Birdie.

"If you really don't mind," I begin, looking over to the couch, "Parker and I will take you up on your offer to crash for the night. You might have a bed buddy, though, because I don't think we'll both fit on the couch."

"Don't be dumb," she says, popping two ibuprofens into her mouth. "Come to bed."

"Are you sure?" I question, narrowing my eyes. I'm all for sharing a bed with Birdie, but this is her space. "I don't mind sleeping on the couch."

"Stop being such a gentleman." She points down the hallway. "Let's go."

"Yes, ma'am," I say, but I know this is a bad idea. I should sleep on the couch. I should go home. "Lead the way."

BIRDIE 23.

I DON'T KNOW what I was thinking inviting Atticus to spend the night in bed with me. It sounded good as I said it, but now that I'm standing here with the dilemma of how I'm supposed to fall asleep with pants on... I don't think I've slept in anything other than a T-shirt and my underwear since college.

I must be wearing my perplexity on my face, because Atticus asks if I'm okay.

"Yeah. I just didn't think this all the way through," I admit.

"I can still go sleep on the couch," he offers, looking down at Parker. "Though you may have a bedmate anyway."

"No, no." Our couch isn't exactly the most comfortable thing in the world. Campbell and I keep saying we're going to replace it, but we just haven't yet. It's one thing for me to have a sore back from sleeping on the floor with Parker. I'm not the one that has to do physical stunts. I can live with a knot in my neck or a tight muscle, Atticus, however, cannot. "You can stay in here. I just usually sleep in a T-shirt and underwear only. I can't remember the last time I slept with pants on. It's going to be weird."

Without a word, he pulls off his gray V-neck T-shirt before dropping it to the floor. I spent six years drooling over those abs from my couch while he was on *Sunset Heights*, but nothing would have prepared me for seeing his half-naked body in person. I try and fail not to make it obvious that I'm gawking at his perfectly chiseled stomach muscles.

"I don't sleep with a shirt on." He grins. "What side of the bed do you sleep on?"

When words fail me, I point to my side of the bed. While he pulls the covers down, I strip out of the leggings I'd been wearing. I unhook my bra from underneath my shirt, then pull the shoulder straps off one by one until I can pull it out from the bottom of my shirt.

Again, something I haven't done since before college.

Normally, I would change into one of my longer sleep shirts, but there's no way I'm taking my shirt off too.

Once we're both under the covers, I expect Parker to jump up and join us, but instead, he circles a few times by the bedroom door and plops down right in front of it.

When we were standing in the kitchen, I was so exhausted I thought I was going to fall over. The emotional toll of feeling helpless as Parker shook from fear during the storm, and the physical toll of sleeping on the cold kitchen floor left me stripped of energy. But as soon as I got into my bed with Atticus, I became hyperaware of his presence.

"Atticus? Are you still awake?" I whisper, turning to face him.

When I see the gentle rise and fall of his body, I don't expect him to answer, but a soft laugh leaves his lips.

"Yeah," he whispers back. "You okay?"

"Tell me something I should know."

"I really want to kiss you right now," he says, and I'd be

willing to swear on everything holy that my heart skips a beat at his admission.

I stare back at him, and it's as if Jette's super-powered energy pulses between us in this moment. It's electric. Terrifying.

And fucking mesmerizing.

I'm held captive by his gaze. The Peter Parker to my Mary Jane is looking back at me in the dark, and in this particular moon-light, as he inches closer, it doesn't feel like an act.

I don't hesitate to close the little distance that's left between us. For eight years, I've wondered what it might be like for those actresses to get the chance to kiss him on screen. This right here is mine. Only now, no one is watching.

His lips find mine like they've been desperate for this all night. My eyes close in response, my mouth opening to his.

He grips my hair and pauses to release a heavy sigh, and my breathing is as erratic as my emotions. I don't want him to stop.

Oh my God. I don't want him to stop.

I allow my hands to wander over his shoulders, down his arms. To the abdomen I've admired under bright lights.

"Atticus?" I whisper.

"Yeah, Birdie," he says, eyes begging.

"I need you to fuck me like I'm your girlfriend."

With that, he tugs me toward him until we're positioned as he pleases. He's hovering just above me, his hair tickling my face, that too-perfect smile a complete tease in and of itself. "Then I'm gonna need you to know that you're mine," he says.

I don't get a chance to respond or determine if he's kidding before his lips find mine again. And those aren't the only lips he finds once he crawls down my body beneath the sheets.

For approximately four or five—I don't know, I lost count—deliriously incredible orgasms in a row, he doesn't just make me feel like I'm his; I *am* his. And he makes damn sure of it.

The final one of the night comes after he demands that I do. In the sexiest, raspiest voice I've ever heard.

And all I can think afterward is: he *definitely* fucks better than Cash. Maybe he just wanted to prove it.

But I'd be lying if I said I didn't enjoy it.

ATTICUS 24.

A DEEP BARK stirs me from a sound sleep. I'm not sure what time Birdie and I crashed. Keeping time was the very last of my priorities.

Sitting up, a smile tugs at my lips when Birdie's little giggle and a "Shh" follows Parker's bark.

"You're going to wake your dad up," she whispers outside the door. "Come on, bud."

"I'm already up," I call out to her. Pulling my pants on and grabbing my shirt, I sprint out of her bedroom. "Birdie. Hold up. I'll take him out."

Joining them in the kitchen, I find Parker happily munching on one of the treats.

"Morning," she greets me, reaching into one of their cabinets. "Well, afternoon. It's after noon. We already went on a walk. I gave him a few of the treats my mom made. I almost went and grabbed him dog food, but I know you make his special. I didn't want to mess that up."

A small pang of guilt hits me. I should have brought him food.

I was so concerned about getting them off the kitchen floor last night that I didn't think past it.

"I know you have things to do today, so we won't stay long," I tell her, taking the mug of coffee she hands me and immediately placing it on the open counter next to us.

"Two sugars, no cream," she says. "That's how you drink it, right?"

"Yes," I assure her before closing the space between us. Running my hands up her back with the slightest amount of pressure, I ask how she feels.

"A little sore," she admits. "I already took a couple—"

Her words stop when she lets out a small moan, her breath slow and deep as I make my way from her shoulder blades to her shoulders.

"You keep making noises like that, and we're going to end up back in the bedroom," I say.

"I've got time."

I've been waiting for a moment like this my whole life. A girl like this, with that kind of smile, who'd appreciate this very thing.

"Yeah?" I counter. "How much time?" I hoist her up over my shoulder, playfully smacking her ass in the process.

Maybe I'm a little too into this role she's cast me in, but she lets out more giggles as I lead us back to the bedroom.

It's not long before those giggles become whimpers. Before she's saying my name and, for the first time in so long, I don't mind hearing it called out repeatedly.

Fake or not, this woman can call me whatever the hell she wants.

BIRDIE 25.

GIRLS' nights at Zoe's have created some of my most favorite memories of all of us together. Growing up, I always wanted a sister. Campbell came pretty close to the real thing. When I was in college, I interned at a big comic publisher in Boston, and that's where I met Nova. She took me under her wing and the rest, as they say, is history.

As the baby of the group, I went from having no siblings to being the little sister to not only Campbell, Nova, Zoe, Francie, Ramona, and Margot, but to Isaac, Bishop, and Beckett—the store manager of the Maine store—too.

I love the guys, but the *Suffra-Jette* sisterhood is one of the most important things to me, even more so than the comic itself. Getting to be a bridesmaid at Nova and Bishop's wedding, being "Auntie B" to Zoe's daughter and Ramona's son, celebrating Margot's engagement last fall, and our annual Galentine's Day movie night and cookie swap at Christmas time—I love spending time with my girls.

And then every once in a while, we get nights like tonight, when we don't have a reason to get together other than being together. There's no need to worry about sales numbers and storylines. We can gossip about guys like teenagers and just be *friends* without the added bonus of being co-workers. In addition to the *Suffra-Jette* crew, Zoe's childhood best friend, Gabriella, will be there. She doesn't work for the comic shop, but she's more or less one of us anyway.

Normally, Campbell and I ride up together, each of us taking turns being the designated driver, but Campbell was gone before Atticus and I left the bedroom this morning. She left a note saying she was heading to the office to get some work done and would meet me at Zoe's later. I haven't talked to her yet, but I wouldn't be surprised to find out that she only left to give Atticus and I some space when she realized we were in the bedroom together.

I laugh, answering the call. "Does Parker miss me already?"

He chuckles. "I mean, probably. But that's not why I'm calling. I know you're on your way to Zoe's for the night, but I really would feel better about booking you a massage. Does tomorrow work? I wanted to take you out for a date, but we can reschedule that."

"You're not going to let this go, are you?"

He's already mentioned the fact I spent hours on the cold kitchen floor multiple times since last night. I'm sore, but mostly from getting properly fucked for the first time in... well, ever. I'm not dogging on anyone else's, erm, performance abilities, but it's never been like *that*.

"Nope."

"Okay, fine," I concede. "But if I go, it's going to be in the morning, and then we're going to go on a date I plan tomorrow afternoon."

"Deal," he agrees. "Do you have a preferred spa close to you?"

I've never gotten a professional massage before, so I tell him the place that Campbell goes to downtown. She has tried to get me to go with her countless times, but I could never justify spending hundreds of dollars to have a stranger rub my body.

"Okay, perfect. I'll take care of it when I get home," Atticus says. And though I can't see him, I can hear his smile growing through the phone. "Have fun with the girls tonight. I'll be around if you want to send out any tipsy texts."

"Noted." I laugh. "Bye, Atticus."

We end the call, and I put on my Hopeless Romantic playlist. It's the playlist I usually listen to when I need to write about Jette and Otto's relationship. Their love is fictional, but it's everything I would want. They're a team in every aspect of the word. They're willing to compromise. They believe in and empower each other, even when everything else in their worlds are falling apart, there's no questioning the love they share. Sometimes, it really is Jette and Otto against the world.

I thought I was fine just creating fictional love, but the way the world spins faster when Atticus kisses me, and how my stomach flutters at just the sound of his voice, I know, without any uncertainty, that this is no longer just pretend.

And I have a two-hour drive to figure out how I'm going to bring this up to Atticus.

I have real feelings for you, fake boyfriend.

Thankfully, I'm headed to Zoe's. There are seven women who will be more than willing to help me figure this shit out.

The woods of New Hampshire will always be home to me, but if I were to *have* to move anywhere else, I think I would choose Lupine Cove, Maine. The coastal Maine town where Zoe and Isaac live—which also happens to be the home of the office and flagship, Coolidge Comics & Collectables—reminds me of a summer Hallmark movie. Quaint small shops fill an ever-bustling Main Street. A salty breeze rolls in from the ocean, just miles from the center of town. It's the kind of place where everyone knows everyone. I'm just a once or twice a month visitor, and even I get greeted by name in most of the places around town at this point.

I left a little early so I could make a stop at the comic shop. I always try to sneak in every once in a while with my sharpie and sign a few random copies of *Suffra-Jette* on the shelves and browse through the dollar bins for any hidden gems.

Before I stop into the store, I head a few doors down to Brew La La to grab a latte. The man behind the counter looks up when the little bell on the door announces my arrival.

"Birdie!" Tyler, Gabriella's husband, greets me with an enthusiastic wave and a bright smile. "Iced London Fog Latte?"

"Yes, please." I nod, impressed he remembers my drink order. "Hey, do you know who is over at the store?"

"Beckett came in this morning. I think Bishop might still be over there too," he says, scooping ice. "You didn't hear it from me, but they're meeting with a new artist today."

"Oooh. I wonder who it is," I ponder aloud. "Hey, can you also make whatever Beckett and Bishop have been drinking lately too?"

Tyler grins before grabbing three cups from a stack on the counter. "You got it."

Over the next few minutes, Tyler asks me questions about *Suffra-Jette*, both the comic and the movie. He's always been one of our biggest supporters.

"What do I owe you?" I ask when he places the last drink into the carrying tray.

Tyler shakes his head. "It's on the house. It's not every day we get a celebrity in here."

"Act like I don't come in here every time I'm in town." I roll my eyes, opening my wallet. Dropping a twenty in the tip jar, I shake my head. "And I didn't just get a drink for me."

"Say hi to Gabriella for me!" He winks, waving me off.

I turn and almost flip the whole tray onto the woman standing abnormally close behind me. I try to make it a habit not to judge someone based on their appearance, but I can't help but notice the messy bun of bleach blonde hair sitting atop her head. Dark circles of exhaustion sit under her big brown eyes, but the most surprising thing is the *Suffra-Jette* graphic tee she has on. It's faded and tattered—much like my favorite Spider-Man shirt that I've had since I was nineteen—but *Suffra-Jette* is only a few years old. If I didn't know better, I might think it was vintage.

"I like your shirt," I tell her, adjusting the cups in the tray. Luckily, nothing fell over or spilled.

"I'm—I'm so sorry." She stammers her apology.

"You good, Birdie?" Tyler calls out.

"Yeah," I say, holding up the tray. "Nothing spilled. Thanks again, Tyler."

I push the door open with my hip and walk two doors over to the comic shop. Just like at Brew La La, a little doorbell chimes when I walk in.

Beckett greets me with a smile and a wave while helping a customer. Looking down to the tray of drinks, I head to the front register and drop his off before walking to the back of the store where the office is.

It's a straight shot to the back, but I'm cut off abruptly by someone coming out of one of the aisles. I open my mouth to apologize because, to be honest, I wasn't exactly expecting anyone to pop out at me.

A small, awkward chuckle leaves my lips when I see it's the same woman from Brew La La.

I laugh nervously. "We really need to stop running into each other like this."

When I step out of the way, I can see the sitting area. It's my favorite part of the store. Two plush couches, a few beanbag chairs, and a stack of free comics are scattered across the coffee table in the middle of it all.

Before Isaac owned the store, it belonged to Calvin Coolidge —the store's namesake. I never got the honor of meeting him, but from the stories Isaac and Zoe have told us, he would have been one of my favorite humans if I had. Much like Nova did for me, Mr. Coolidge took a young Isaac under his wing and taught him everything he knew. It's because Mr. Coolidge took a leap of faith in hiring the quiet, shy kid who came into his store every week to buy comics that we're all here today.

A small boy, who can't be more than seven or eight, pulls my attention to one of the couches. I don't know if I've just watched too many episodes of Criminal Minds, but the woman walking around pops into my head.

"Do we know who the kid on the couch belongs to?" I ask Beckett when I find him by himself at the counter.

"He's mine," a gruff voice booms from behind me. "Is everything alright?"

Broad shoulders, a face full of freckles, and deep red hair that belongs to illustrator Torsten Beck.

Torsten and I went to high school together. He was a senior when I was a freshman and would have absolutely no clue who I am, but my mom asks me all the time if I know him. In true Annie Yamamoto fashion, she managed to connect the dots and has become friends with his mother.

Torsten and I have never crossed paths until now, despite having remarkably comparable stories. After college, we both ended up working for the same comic book company I started at in Boston. He left before I got there, though. Last I heard, according to my mother, he was working for DC Comics on a Harley Quinn series.

Lowering my voice, I tell him about the woman walking around. "I'm sure she's harmless. I just got worried seeing him all by himself."

"Shit," he mutters under his breath before sighing. "I'm supposed to have a meeting with Bishop, but my babysitter fell through. I've already had to cancel on him twice, so I figured bringing him would be better than not showing up."

"I know we just met, but I don't mind hanging out for a bit on the other couch," I tell him. "Beckett and Bishop can vouch for me. I'm Birdie—"

The corner of Torsten's lips curls up. "Yamamoto. I know who you are. I'm—"

Taking my own turn, I laugh and finish for him. "Torsten Beck. I know who you are too."

"Just Tor." His face softens a bit when he looks over at the little boy lazily lounging on the couch, flipping through the pages of a comic book. "And that's Ollie. If you really don't mind hanging out with him, I would owe you one."

"You wouldn't owe me anything."

I've definitely been saying that to men too often lately. Once I get back to the sitting area, I grab the first comic in reach.

"Hi, Ollie. I'm Birdie. I'm going to hang out here with you while your dad meets with Mr. Vaughn," I say, plopping down on the couch across from Ollie. With my introduction, he looks up to his dad for confirmation, and all it takes is the curt nod from his father to reassure him that I'm okay. "Whatcha reading?"

He holds up a copy of *Thor (2020)*. I recognize the issue based on the cover art—multiple characters with their hands on Mjölnir, Thor's infamous hammer—and try to remember what exactly happens in the story.

"My dad said Thor is Norse, like us." I don't know what's cuter—Ollie's toothless grin or his pride in relating to the god of thunder himself. "And Loki too. Dad says I'm a lot like him."

"The god of mischief," I note, nodding in approval. "He's one of my favorites."

"You read comic books?" Ollie asks with such disbelief in his voice that I can't help but laugh. "I've never met a girl that likes to read comic books. All the girls at school read books like *Dork Diaries*."

"Not only do I read them but I write them too," I tell him. "Wanna see? I bet we can find a copy or two around here somewhere."

BIRDIE 26.

AN HOUR AND A HALF LATER, I say goodbye to my new friend Ollie and make my way across town to the Adams' residence.

Pulling up to the house, I break out into a smile when I see a brunette toddler-sized version of Zoe running across the front lawn with her head tipped back in laughter.

"Gwen Stacy Adams," Zoe calls, running out the front door. "You bring that cute little butt back here and give me a kiss goodnight."

At the sight of Zoe's older brother, Charlie, waiting on the lawn next door, I realize I arrived just as Gwen is making her way over to Zoe's parents' house for a sleepover of her own. The sound of my car door shutting grabs Gwen's attention and causes her to stop midsprint. Her eyes widen with excitement as she waves at me.

"Auntieee Birdieee!"

"Gwen!" I exclaim. Before I have the chance to open the back door of my car to grab the wine I brought, I'm bent down, scooping a three-year-old into my arms.

"Mama said your superhewo book is going to be a movie! That's sooo cool."

"It is pretty cool, huh?" I agree with her as she squeezes me as tightly as her little arms will allow.

She doesn't answer me, because Charlie laughs and says, "Oh, I get it. Uncle Charlie is chopped liver when Auntie Birdie is around. I'll remember that next time you want ice cream before dinner."

At that, Gwen wiggles to get out of my arms, and I place her back down on the grass below.

"Not so fast, little lady!" Zoe grabs onto her and loads her face with kisses.

The little giggles that come from Gwen as her mother peppers her face with love are quite possibly the purest sound I've ever heard. While they say their goodbyes for the night, I retrieve the wine from my back seat and let myself into the house. Due to my impromptu babysitting session at the shop, I'm the last one to arrive.

"Oh, look who made it," Campbell teases when I join everyone in the living room. "Nice to see you and Atticus found your way out of your bedroom."

"Whoa, whoa, whoa," Francie says, holding up her hand. "Wait a damn minute. Does that mean you're, like, a real couple?"

"I don't know," I answer honestly. I'm greeted with seven pairs of eyes calling bullshit on me. "I really don't know where we stand. We had incredible sex last night... and this morning... but we haven't labeled anything. Nothing's changed as far as the arrangement we had."

"What arrangement?" Gabriella asks and I let out a sigh. I forgot she didn't know.

Hanging on to my every word, I give her the condensed version of Atticus and Birdie, a fake love story.

When I finish, she turns to Zoe and smirks. "Sounds a little like someone else I know."

"What?" Ramona exclaims, clearly as shocked as I am.

"Seriously. What?" Margot echoes our surprise.

I'm glad to see I'm not the only one who has no idea what's going on right now.

I don't know what the rest of the team thought, but I always assumed that Zoe and Isaac were just one of those couples that had been together forever. Zoe has never shared much about their past, just that Isaac was her brother's best friend growing up, and the house they live in was handed down to Isaac from his grandmother. And we all know her parents live in the house next door. I honestly thought they were high school sweethearts—or something like that.

"Yeah, Isaac had some girl issues, and he needed someone to pretend to be his girlfriend to settle the busybodies of this town," Zoe starts. "We let it go on longer than we should have when real feelings got involved and, well, you all know how that worked out for us. A business and a baby later…"

"She's being nice." Gabriella shakes her head. "This other woman was on Isaac's nuts. And you know Isaac. He doesn't have a mean bone in his body. He's always been like that. So, because he wouldn't tell her to get lost, she assumed he wanted her. Zoe helped him by pretending to be his girlfriend so this woman would leave Isaac alone."

"I was all about it. I had a crush on Isaac *for-ev-er*," Zoe says before taking a sip of her wine. "No one knew, though. Or at least I thought no one knew. I didn't even tell Gabriella because I was afraid of how weird things would get with him being Charlie's best friend. Turns out my brother knew the whole damn time."

"That sounds like Birdie and Cash." Campbell laughs. A mix of fear, embarrassment, and surprise causes my body to flush with heat from the tips of my toes to my cheeks. "Except Cash knew, and our families all knew, and they just thought we didn't."

"You knew?" I ask in horror. I'd spent so much time and energy keeping it from Campbell and my family.

"I figured you'd tell me if you wanted to." How she can be so nonchalant about it all is completely baffling to me. "I knew you would either end up together or you'd get sick of his shit and move on. It just depended on who smartened up first. It was you. I love my little brother, but even I can admit he's a bit of a fuck-boy." She shakes it off with a laugh before continuing. "But that doesn't matter now. You have Atticus."

"Do I really, though?" I think aloud.

I've been so wrapped up in the idea of Atticus and I creating a fake relationship for the world that I never expected to have real feelings for him. There's also a nagging worry that this may all just be Atticus getting swept up in the process of *Suffra-Jette.*

"What happens when the movie is done? When the bubble pops and he realizes he's been fucking around with a chubby comic book writer from New Hampshire? Let's be real now. I can never compete with the likes of any of his exes. Set aside the physical differences, I—"

"Stop." Campbell raises her hand. "Whatever you're thinking, stop. He's crazy about you. Anyone with two eyes can see that. He brought you comic books to sign, and he made sure all of your friends could be with you for your first big date in the public's eyes. And that stint on your parents' deck? You can try to say he wasn't trying to make a point to Cash, but I was there."

"And the way he looks at you." Nova sighs happily. "Even Bishop calls bullshit on the whole it-being-*fake* thing."

"Isaac does too." Zoe agrees. "He said that after the gala. He *actually* said that he hopes you wait to break Atticus's heart until after the movie is done filming."

I scoff. "As if I could break Atticus's heart."

"I don't think you realize just how much power you wield, little bird," Nova says before reaching for my hand.

Such a sisterly thing to say. I knew they would come through with the advice and reassurance.

"So, are we going to talk about the sex yet?" Francie asks, inciting a laugh from everyone. "I bet it was amazing."

"Better than amazing."

ATTICUS 27.

WHILE I WAS on my drive home from Birdie's this afternoon, Bishop called me and asked if I wanted to come over for a last-minute bonfire with some of the guys.

I almost said no. Not because I didn't want to, but because Parker has never been left alone at night. He's fine by himself during the day or for a few hours to grab dinner, but if I'm drinking, I'm certainly not driving home from Maine. Especially when Bishop also offered me the couch, saying, "I would give you the spare bedroom, but Tor and his son are crashing there for the night."

I didn't know who Tor was, but I let Bishop know that as long as I could figure out something for Parker, I was fine with couch crashing.

Parker is a good boy, but I know there's no way he would play nice with Bishop and Nova's two cats.

When I remember that Aunt Bea came home from Florida this morning, I call, bribing her with takeout from her favorite restaurant in town and a Barnes and Noble shopping trip later this week if she'll puppysit for the night. We negotiated takeout and dinner with both me and Birdie instead. Of course, I'm the sucker, because before we end the call, she tells me she would have done it for nothing.

Parker could not care less about me the second he hears that he's going to Aunt Bea's. I'm starting to think I'm second fiddle to the women in my life. Not that I can blame him. Especially when it comes to one certain comic book writer who has been stealing all my thoughts since I left her.

I'm glad she's getting a night to spend with her friends, but selfishly, I wish we could have gone back to my place and continued where we left off this morning. And not just the mind-blowing sex. We need to talk about what's going on. I don't want her to think I'm taking advantage of the situation we're in.

I have a sister. I know girls talk. The thought of her heading to Zoe's and talking about not knowing what's going on between us makes me want to call her right now and put a label on it.

Luckily for me, her friends aren't assholes.

There's something about this crowd of people that sets them apart from any other group of friends I've ever met before. There's so much genuine love. There's no competition—even in a setting where you're trying for the same thing.

I've yet to hear anyone bad-mouth or gossip about another person. Maybe I just need to get out of Los Angeles more. Honestly, since I've been back to film *Suffra-Jette*, the thought of leaving my Massachusetts home to go back to California has felt less and less appealing by the day. The sense of belonging I feel when I'm home is hard to explain to anyone from outside of New England.

By the time I pull up to the address Bishop sent me, there's already a driveway full of cars. Per Bishop's instructions, I let myself in the side gate and make my way to the roaring fire illuminating the yard. I wasn't sure what to expect walking into this boys' night, but I'm relieved to see it's just a handful of guys hanging around a fire and drinking beers.

The sound of my footsteps catches Bishop's attention, and he immediately walks away from the charcoal grill he's standing in front of, taking one of the six-packs of beers I brought before shaking my hand.

He goes around introducing the other guys. Beckett is the manager of the flagship store here in Lupine Cove. Tyler owns the coffee shop a few doors down and is married to Zoe's childhood best friend.

"And this is Tor." He grins, clasping his hand on a redhead's shoulder. "He was specifically requested by Zoe for the variant cover for the next issue of *Suffra-Jette*."

"Ah, I knew I recognized you from somewhere." Tyler's eyes light up in recognition when he looks at me. It immediately gives me a sense of unease. I know, I know. Getting recognized comes with the territory of being an actor, but I've never *not* been completely awkward about it. "You're dating Birdie."

A sense of pride fills me when, of all the things that could have been said, that's what I'm being acknowledged for.

"I am," I confirm with a nod.

"Did you give him the talk?" Beckett asks Bishop, his eyes pointed in my direction.

"He did," I vouch for Bishop. "And so did Isaac, and Campbell, and Zoe, and Nova, and Francie…"

Tyler laughs. "I'd be more worried about the girls than any of us."

"That's what I said," Bishop agrees before taking a swig of his beer and turning toward Tor. "Birdie is the baby of our group. We're all slightly protective of her."

"I can see that." Tor raises his bottle to me. "Godspeed, man."

I take a sip out of my own bottle before taking a seat in one of the empty canvas camping chairs by the fire.

"Actually," I start, looking back and forth between Bishop and Beckett. "Speaking of Birdie, I could use your help with something."

BIRDIE 28.

I SPENT most of the morning teeter-tottering on whether or not this is a smart idea, but as soon as I tell Atticus we're going to the Townsend Children's Home, there's an understanding recognition in his eyes, and I knew I made the right choice.

"I know this won't be as glamorous as a regency ball, but—"

Atticus cuts me off as we walk together toward the front door. "This is just as important as what we were raising money for at the gala."

As soon as I walk through the door, I'm greeted by Betsy Landry. Betsy is the daughter of Jeanette Landry, the founder of the Townsend Children's Home. Jeanette spent her entire childhood in and out of foster homes. When she was just twenty-two, she won the lottery and bought the property the children's home was built on. Betsy followed in her mom's footsteps and took over a couple of years ago when Jeanette retired from running the home full-time.

When I was having a challenging time trying to figure out my identity as an adopted child, my dad brought me to the children's home to talk to Jeanette. For the first time in my life, I had found a kindred spirit. Someone who really understood me. My visits were both therapeutic and eye-opening. It made me realize how lucky I was that Annie and Ken took me into their home and their hearts, but that it was okay to feel a little lost sometimes.

At least once a month, and more if I can swing it, I stop by and volunteer an afternoon. I've helped paint bedrooms, read countless stories, and cooked meals for the twenty or so kids that call this group housing "home."

"Birdie!" Betsy smiles warmly at the sight of me. As soon as Atticus steps into the lobby and finds his place at my side, her eyes widen in surprise. "And you brought a friend."

"Betsy, Atticus. Atticus, Betsy." I'm sure the introduction isn't necessary, but Atticus would be mortified if I made a big deal out of his presence. That's not why we're here. "What can we help with today?"

"Mom and I were just talking about doing something to get these kids out of the house," Betsy says. "It's just too nice to stay inside."

"How about strawberry picking?" I offer. Knowing full well that everything is always well budgeted and planned for, before she can shut down the idea, I add, "My treat."

"I couldn't ask that of you." Betsy shakes her head. "No. As much as I appreciate the offer, we couldn't."

"You didn't ask," I rebut. "You're right. It's too nice. Get those kiddos in the vans. I insist."

"You're too good to us," she says with watery eyes. "You know that?"

"Not every kid has someone like my parents or your mom to look out for them," I say, then remind her that I will always do whatever I can to help.

Once Betsy leaves to find her mom, I turn to Atticus to tell him that he can bail if he wants. Strawberry picking was not on the agenda for the day, but as soon as Betsy started talking, I couldn't help myself. There's a softness in his eyes that I haven't seen before now.

"I'll pay for the strawberries," he offers before I can tell him that I don't expect him to come to the farm. "I *want* to pay for the strawberries."

"How about I pay for the strawberries, and you pay for the lemonade we treat them to after?"

"Deal."

———

THE FARM IS ONLY ABOUT TEN MINUTES FROM THE children's home, so Atticus and I go ahead to give someone a heads-up that there are two vans full of kids on their way and to pre-purchase the containers for picking.

A delectable scent of cinnamon and sweet fruit greets us as soon as we walk into the wooden barn that serves as a store. Almost immediately, people eye us. There's a small tinge of panic that fills me, wondering why everyone would be looking this way, until I remember who I'm here with.

The more time I spend with Atticus, the more I lose sight of his profession—and all that comes with it—and see him as just Atticus. The guy who loves his family and dog more than anything. Except Skittles. For someone who spends two hours a day at the gym and most of his time eating clean, he can throw down a bag of Skittles faster than anyone I've ever seen.

"Hi." Atticus greets the cashier. "We have two vans full of kids coming this way, and I'd like to pay for twenty nine-quart containers for PYO strawberries."

I reach into my back pocket where I stashed my debit card, but before I can, Atticus slides his card into the reader.

"I'd also like to pre-purchase ten gallons of lemonade and four dozen blueberry donuts. You don't happen to have cups here, do you?"

"We don't, sir," the silver-haired woman behind the counter starts. "But if you wouldn't mind letting us take your picture and posting that you both came to visit our farm, I could certainly make sure there were cups here by the time you finished picking. We won't post the photo until after you've left, of course."

"I'll do you one better," Atticus starts. "I'll also make a post that I was here—after we leave, of course—talking about how incredible our experience was."

"Is this a family trip?" she asks as she counts and stacks the pick your own bags on the counter.

"This one"—Atticus nudges me slightly—"volunteers at the Townsend Children's Home every month and decided that the kids needed to go strawberry picking today. It's all the kids currently staying at the children's home."

The older woman stops midgrab and puts her hand up to her heart. "Oh my word. You should have started with that. I wouldn't have taken a penny from you. If you all need anything else while you're here, just ask anyone to find Doris or Chuck. My husband and I own the farm."

Once we've gotten all the bags, Doris follows us outside to take our photo by the farm's sign. With such ease, Atticus pulls me to his side, his fingers lightly gripping my waist. It isn't until this moment that it dawns on me that she requested both of us in the photograph.

After she snaps the picture, she comes and shows us her phone for approval. God, we're cute.

"Do you have pick your own apples too?" I ask, the wheels already spinning in my head for the fall.

As if she's reading my mind, Doris nods. "And we have enough room in the back barn to host a pumpkin painting night. Oh, and we can do a hayride. I'm fairly sure Chuck plans to have a corn maze this year too."

While she has her phone out, I offer my number and ask her to contact me for the best days. I know something like this wouldn't be able to be a last-minute thing like today was, so I tell her that I will coordinate with Betsy and be in touch. Before returning to the store, she reminds us just to ask if we need anything else.

As soon as she's out of earshot, I turn to Atticus. Pinching his arm slightly, I say, "I told you I was going to pay for the strawberries."

I didn't want to cause a scene in the store, but he must have known this was coming. I don't care how many more zeros are in his bank account. This was my idea. My commitment. I didn't expect or want him to feel like he needed to pay for anything.

"Ouch." He laughs and then points to the two vans as they pull into the dirt parking lot. "Oh, look. The kids are here."

"I'm going to pay you back for that. One way or another."

Whether he likes it or not.

"Is this our first fight?" he asks, then leans in closer so that only I can hear him. "You know what they say—the best part about fighting is making up afterward."

As a trail of goose bumps slide up my arms, I gently push him away. "You're trouble."

"You don't even know the half of it yet."

ATTICUS 29.

I COULD SAY that I slid my hand into Birdie's for the sake of keeping up appearances.

I *could* say that, but I'd be lying. The truth is, every single second spent with her makes me wonder how long I'm going to be able to sit here and pretend that what we have, what I feel, isn't real.

As much as I would love to think that I paid for everything as a selfless thing for the kids, it was a decision equally fueled by the fact that I knew doing something like that would matter to Birdie. I didn't want the credit. I didn't need anyone else to know it was me that took care of everything. But I wanted Birdie to know if it's important to her, it's important to me.

It's been a long time—so long that I don't remember the last time—that I've desperately wanted to let someone in beyond the wall I built when I realized that with fame and money comes a lot of people wanting to be in your life for all the wrong self-serving reasons. Whether it be asking to "borrow" money or using my name as a stepping-stone for whatever they're reaching for, I've learned the hard way that some people are really good at pretending to give a shit to get what they want.

But then, there's Birdie. The girl that brings breakfast for the crew and sleeps on cold, hard kitchen floors with my dog. The girl that fights for the check every time and wishes romance, real romance, wasn't just something found in the Jane Austen books she secretly loves so much.

At this point, there's no sense in denying that I feel something for Birdie. At first, I thought I just wanted what I couldn't have. She hated me. But once she stopped hating me and started letting me see the girl hiding behind the angry eyes and quick jabs to my ego, I knew it was more than that.

"Earth to Atticus."

A hand slowly waves in front of my face, snapping me back to the present. "Sorry." I chuckle, turning to Birdie. Her pinched, raised brows settle back into place as her lips curl into a small smile when I give her my attention. "I had one too many beers at Bishop's last night. Maybe I should go grab one of those maple lattes inside."

"You were at Bishop's last night?" she questions.

"I was," I confirm. "He had a bonfire with a couple of the guys."

"Huh."

Huh. That's it. There is no emotion in her voice that could give an inkling of what that one little word means, and I don't have time to ask before a group of kids come running toward us.

A boy with bright red hair and a face full of freckles eyes me suspiciously. It's the same look I get at grocery stores. The *I know you from somewhere but can't place where* look.

"Atticus and Birdie, how about you guys take off with the teens?" Betsy suggests when she joins us. "We'll wrangle the rest of these hooligans."

There are only three teenagers. All three of them are girls.

"I think we can handle that." Birdie smiles, handing a bag to each of the girls and then to me. Leading the way into the orchard, the girls follow behind her and I follow behind them.

"Kallie, Lily, and Emily, this is Atticus." One by one, Birdie introduces me to the girls. "Atticus, this is Kallie, Lily, and Emily."

Either none of them know who I am or they just don't give a shit. And it's amazing.

"I also happen to be Birdie's boyfriend," I say, winking at Birdie.

I know this isn't somewhere we need to make our "relationship" known, and that's what makes it all that much more important that they do. This isn't an act or a game to me anymore. I want everyone to know.

"There's a ton over there," Kallie says, pointing to a vine a few rows over.

"You girls go ahead. We'll catch up," Birdie tells them. As soon as they're out of earshot, she turns to me. "You didn't have to do that. Not here."

"I know," I assure her, reaching down for a bright red strawberry. "This looks like it'll be a good one."

"Atticus, I'm being serious." She frowns. "These girls don't need to think you're going to be back again. If they think you're my boyfriend, they'll want to see you. I know you can't commit to that. I just don't want to be a source of disappointment for them."

"I'll come back," I swear.

Sighing, she starts to walk toward the group of teenagers. "Don't make promises you can't keep."

BIRDIE 30.

I KNEW this day was coming. It had to come eventually. Atticus is playing Jette's love interest for goodness' sake. What I wasn't ready for was the way my stomach twisted when I watched him pull Violet into his arms and kiss her. I didn't expect my heart to feel like it was going to slam out of my chest when their lips touched. Again. And again. And again.

We left things in a weird place yesterday. Or, really, I made things weird yesterday. After we were done picking strawberries, Atticus gave me a ride back to my car at the children's home. He asked me out to dinner, and I declined, claiming that I was exhausted and needed to go to bed early.

Not only did I not go to bed early but I also spent most of the night thinking of every reason this thing wouldn't work between the two of us. If I figured out every way things could go wrong, I could avoid them all and save myself from getting hurt.

But then I come here today, and I'm fucking jealous. It's just acting. He's doing his job right now. But seeing his lips on another woman incites a kind of rage I've never felt before.

It's a PG-13 movie and I helped write the script, so I know there won't be anything explicit coming from this scene, but after the eighth take of them kissing, if I don't get the fuck out of there, I'm going to cause a commotion. After my first little outburst on day one of filming, I've done everything to stay in the background.

I highly doubt Atticus, the director, the crew, and Violet especially, would appreciate me throwing the orange I brought at Violet's head like I want to.

After grabbing my notebook and my phone, I quietly tiptoe off set. By the time I get outside, I find myself gasping for air.

"Damn it!" I curse under my breath as soon as I'm outside. "Shit. Shit. Shit."

Lately, I've been spending time with Atticus in his trailer in between filming, but being in close proximity to him right now will only lead to me admitting things I don't care to admit.

I could go to the *Suffra-Jette* team trailer, but that will be the next place he looks for me. Fight or flight kicks in and leaves me with no option. I need to get the fuck out of here. The last time this kind of panic set in was after the table read when I thought he was an egotistical piece of shit. And now here I am, running from my feelings again.

But unlike the last time, I have plans with Atticus in forty-eight hours. Which means I have two days to get my emotions in check. I have two days to refocus. Readjust. This is a business deal; a means to promote the movie. This is not real. We went too far by being intimate with each other. That needs to stop too.

At the end of the day, all arrangements aside, Atticus isn't mine. We aren't together. He can kiss whoever the hell he wants.

That doesn't change the fact that I spend the entire forty-five-minute drive back to my house imagining what it would have been like to see the orange smash open on Violet's forehead. Poor Violet. She's completely innocent in all of this. And, the truth is, I adore her.

She's been nothing but nice to me since we first met. And yet, here I am, envisioning a situation where the sting of the orange juice in her eyes would stop them from completing the kiss scene. I'm an asshole. An asshole that needs to clear her aura and recenter.

Campbell is in Maine for the day with Zoe and Nova, so I have the house to myself. More often than not, Campbell's presence is reassuring, but today, I'm thankful to have the space to breathe and not have to worry about bothering her while I blast music.

In an effort to cleanse the nasty thoughts, I immediately head for the shower. My mom gifted me lavender shower steamers that are meant to relax you, so I toss one of them into the bathtub and turn the water temperature as hot as my skin can handle. Campbell must have changed the setting on the showerhead, because the pressure as the water hits my skin is almost painful, but in the good, healing way. I didn't realize my shoulders were so tense from the stress of watching Atticus…

Nope. I'm done doing this.

As the scalding water massages my skin, I close my eyes and take a breath. I reach for the eucalyptus and tea tree body oil, then wash my body for the second time today. This time has nothing to do with cleansing my skin, though. This time is all about cleansing my thoughts.

To shift my focus on something else, I tell the speaker we keep in the bathroom—which is connected to the service I use for streaming music—to play Sammy Rae and The Friends. The universe must acknowledge my need for a pick-me-up, because "Jackie Onassis" begins to play. Using the bottle of body wash as my microphone, I sing along, swaying to the sound of the soothing, steady drumbeat.

When I'm done, I dry off and put lotion on my legs, arms, and stomach before sliding a sundress over my head. I toyed with not putting on any clothing. The opportunity to walk around the house butt ass naked rarely presented itself, but I can't meditate naked.

It's not to say I haven't tried, but the entire time I should have been focusing on my home base and, you know, clearing my mind, all I could think about how my boobs rose and fell with every breath I took.

Plopping down on the yoga mat still in the middle of my bedroom from this morning, I sigh when I realize I'm going to need to get my phone to access the app I use for guided meditation. Hopefully, one day I'll be able to meditate without needing someone to tell me what to do every step of the way, but for now, guided meditation works.

On the way back down to the kitchen, where I tossed my phone and notebook, I decide that meditation can wait a bit longer, when I remember that I my mom stopped by with fresh tomatoes and basil from her garden. Knowing we wouldn't have it in the house, she also brought white bread and Miracle Whip.

Listen, okay, I *know* most people are on Team Mayo when it comes to the mayonnaise versus Miracle Whip argument, but I will forever stand by my opinion that Miracle Whip is the better of the two—especially on tomato sandwiches.

Tomato sandwiches are easily one of my favorite things about summer. Even the most gourmet of meals can't compete with thick slices of vine-ripened tomatoes, a sprinkle of basil, and an unhealthy amount of Miracle Whip on some cheap, store-bought white bread.

According to my baby book, "mato" was even one of my first words.

Once I prepare my sandwich, I reach for my phone to take a picture to send to my mom. My excitement over my sandwich allowed me a temporarily, albeit short-lived, reprieve of Atticus Cohen flooding my thoughts. Those fleeting moments are gone when I look on my lock screen to see a missed call and a text alert —both of them from Atticus.

Knowing I can't avoid him forever, I tap on the little phone icon to call him back. "Hey. I was just thinking about you."

Oh really? That's cool. Because I've been thinking about you too. Nonstop actually.

I manage to force out a small laugh. "Oh yeah?"

"Is everything all right? I looked up and you were just gone. I looked everywhere you could be. My trailer. The *Suffra-Jette* team trailer. Food services. The Brew La La tent. And then when you didn't answer your calls or your texts, I started to worry…"

I don't tell him that I silenced my phone when I walked into the house so there was no way I would have heard him calling.

"Sorry," I apologize. A small wave of guilt washes over me when I hear the worry in his voice. "I just had some stuff to take care of at home and you were, um, busy. I should have let you know I was leaving."

He doesn't need to know that the things I needed to "take care of" included burning the memory of him and Violet kissing from my brain so I could move on with my life.

"So you're home?" he questions. "Because I just happen to be in the neighborhood. I have a London Fog Iced Latte and a blueberry scone with your name on it."

"You just *happen* to be in the neighborhood?" I repeat.

There's nothing in the neighborhood for him—except me. The only other people he knows in Townsend are Campbell, Cash, and my parents. Campbell isn't in town, he's not close enough to my parents, and the very last person I would picture Atticus making plans with is Cash Porter.

"Yep," he says. "Are you going to let me in? Or should I eat these scones on your front steps?"

ATTICUS 31.

"YOU CHANGED," I note as we walk into the kitchen. "You were wearing pants and a Spider-Man T-shirt before."

"Yeah. I took a shower," she says. "Why are you here, Atticus?"

"What's going on?" I ask her. "What's *really* going on? I saw you run off set. You didn't say goodbye. Which is fine, but then you weren't answering my calls or my texts."

I've spent enough time with her to know that when something or someone is bothering her, she avoids them. That's what she did with me when she thought I was an asshole. I have a feeling she left because she was uncomfortable watching me kiss Violet over and over again, and the fact that she won't even look at me right now is even more telling.

"You kissed her." Her voice is so low and timid that it's barely recognizable as hers. Shaking her head, she continues, her voice growing stronger with every word. "I get it. It's your job. It's in the script—the one I helped write, for fuck's sake. I know it's irrational, and I have no right to be mad or jealous or whatever the fuck this is that I'm feeling, but you kissed her and all I could think about was throwing the orange I was holding at her head."

A loud laugh booms from my chest. I was expecting her to tell me that the kiss bothered her. I wasn't expecting her to tell me she wanted to throw an orange at Violet's head.

"What are you even doing here?" she fumes, opening the fridge with enough force that the door whips backward. "And don't give me some bullshit that you were 'in the neighborhood.' The only other people you know in this town are my parents and Cash."

Gently, I reach for the tomatoes in her hand before putting them down on the table behind me.

"I didn't come to see your parents."

She doesn't finish her thought as my hands cup her face.

"But I'm sure Cash could use some reminding," I tell her, half kidding.

She scrunches her face and scoffs. "Reminding of what, exactly?"

I shrug, moving some of her hair away from her gorgeous face. "That you're mine."

She looks down briefly. "Atticus. Stop. This isn't funny anymore."

I wipe that laugh off her lips with a feverish kiss. One way hotter and way more authentic than that bullshit kiss with Violet I'd been obligated to do via contract and duty.

I lift her onto the counter, and then my hands find her thighs. As her head tips back, her hands around my neck, I lean into hers, peppering kisses along the sensitive spot.

"I'm not trying to be funny," I whisper against her skin.

She strips her shirt off and hops down from the counter. Then we're both removing each other's clothes in a hurried blur between kisses.

Finally, I pin her against the wall, skin to skin, chest to heaving chest. And all I can think is that I hope she knows how much I meant that. How much I mean *this*.

BiRDiE 32.

"OKAY, so I have to admit something," Atticus starts. "I did have another reason for coming here."

"Which was?" I ask.

"Do you know how Ryder hosts lunches every now and then? Well, he just asked me to help him get the *Suffra-Jette* girls together for a late lunch around three o'clock. I called Zoe. She was with Nova and Campbell already, and she said she would call the other girls too. I just need to convince you."

"So that's what this was?" My stomach drops. "You just did all that to convince me to have lunch with Ryder? A text would have been sufficient."

"A text would have been sufficient if that was the only thing I needed to tell you," he says.

"There's more?" I groan.

"What would you say if I told you I didn't want to do this anymore?" Atticus questions. "This fake relationship."

"I would say I was right to assume you're an asshole all along."

Heat rises under my skin. I hate how he can easily throw my body off balance from one extreme to the other. I was just frozen in his arms, unable to move after he fucked me against the wall, and now he doesn't want to do this anymore?

He reaches for my hand. "I don't want to be in a fake relationship anymore because it doesn't *feel* fake. It feels real. I want this to be real."

"What exactly are you saying, Atticus?"

I don't want to misconstrue what he's implying. I don't know how I could, but after I fucked up at the table read, I've learned that clarification is necessary when it comes to Atticus.

"Be my girlfriend? With no hidden agenda. No trying to get the media's attention. Just us. You and me. For real."

As much as I want to listen to the fluttering burst of emotions that are telling me to say yes, the thoughts in my head are louder.

"Are you sure?" I ask. "What happens when the movie is over? Then what?"

"I'll take a break. Book another movie. I might have to travel, but you'll be working on the comic." He says it like he's got it all figured out already. "We can video chat. You could visit me on set."

"It sounds like you've given this some thought." I straighten my dress as he lets out a laugh.

"I knew before I even met you that you were going to change my life," Atticus begins. "I had no idea just how much, though. Everything we've done in the duration of this fake relationship has been out of my own want. I want to be around you. I miss you when I'm not. Getting to know you and be a part of your world with you and your friends has been the best part of this movie experience. I don't want that to end when filming does."

"You don't need me to be friends with Isaac and Bishop," I tell him. "And we can—"

"Don't you say it." His lips form a thin, straight line as he shakes his head. "Don't you dare say we can still be friends. I don't want to be your friend, Birdie. Not when I know what it feels like to be more than that."

I don't want to be *just* his friend either. That became perfectly clear to me and everyone else when I couldn't handle seeing him kiss another woman.

Everything about Atticus and I defies all logic, though that's pretty on par for this experience as a whole.

Suffra-Jette was my first comic book as lead writer. Her story is mine. Isaac and Zoe have created such an incredible place for us, but they don't have the number like bigger names. Or... they didn't. The likelihood of seeing the success we have is almost unheard of. We got here with an abundance of good luck.

Writers of all genres dream of having their work up on the big screen. Some people write dozens of books and have been doing so for longer than I've been alive, and yet, less than five years after the very idea of *Suffra-Jette* was born, we're here.

I am here. Right now. With Atticus. Because of a million little things that had to happen just the way they did.

And I would be foolish to deny that I want every little bit of what he's offering right now.

"Okay," I tell him.

I could produce a slew of reasons why this won't work between us. But I don't want to fight it anymore. Not even a little bit.

"Okay?" Atticus repeats back to me. "What exactly are you saying, Birdie?"

What a brat.

"Let's do this," I say as the corners of his lips curl into a smile. "Let's do this for real."

He closes the space between us and pulls me to him. Just when I think we're going to seal the deal with a kiss, Atticus groans.

"I really want to kiss you right now, but I know if I start, we're not going to stop until we're naked again." Before he steps back, he gently plants a kiss on my forehead. "I don't jump when many people tell me to, but Ryder Donegan Jr. is expecting you for lunch."

I should put on panties and a bra. It feels a little risqué to be in Ryder's presence without them. I am one hundred and ten percent for women freely expressing their sexuality, but a luncheon with a Hollywood icon doesn't feel like a place I need to display my goodies.

HAND IN HAND, ATTICUS AND I APPROACH A LARGE white tent bigger than the entire *Suffra-Jette* team trailer. It's no secret that everyone is accommodating Ryder because of his legacy. I haven't heard him asking for any special treatment, but he's getting it nonetheless.

His weekly lunches have become infamous around the set. Atticus has been lucky enough to attend two of them. He came back from the last one with a sore stomach because he overindulged in fresh salmon cakes. I never thought I would get an invite of my own, though.

I couldn't bring myself to look Ryder in the eyes at the table read. Then, when shit hit the fan with Atticus, my hatred became tunnel vision. I haven't been able to bring myself to talk to him since. Even after going to the gala and being around Atticus every day since, I cannot shake the anxiety that fills me when I think of approaching Ryder.

The worst part is that he hasn't done anything to warrant such feelings. He isn't on set trying to make friends with everyone the way Violet and Atticus are, but he's never been mean or rude to anyone either. His presence is intimidating—unintentionally, but still intimidating.

When we approach the opening of the tent, the soft sound of classical music greets us.

"Birdie. You made it," Ryder exclaims, stepping out from the inside. Atticus leans over to give me a kiss goodbye and Ryder laughs. "Oh, stop it. You can stay too, Atticus."

"You don't have to tell me twice." An ear-to-ear smile settles on Atticus's face.

Stepping inside the tent, swirls of vanilla and maple surround us. It's three o'clock in the afternoon. I didn't know what to expect, but a long table full of breakfast food certainly wasn't it.

"Breakfast." I grin, looking up at Ryder. "How did you know that's my favorite?"

"Your boyfriend seems to know you well," he answers with a smile of his own. "We haven't had a breakfast-themed lunch yet —I'm excited."

Ryder rattles off the food options, but I'm only half listening. Because this is when it hits me. Like, really hits me. I've been floating on the high of everything going on, and I haven't accepted this is actually happening. And not just lunch with Ryder—but everything. All of it.

"Hey there." Ryder waves his hand slowly in front of my face. "Are you okay, darling?"

"I'm sorry," I apologize. The flush of warmth on my cheeks is a good indicator that my embarrassment is visible on my face as well. "This is incredible. Thank you so much for including us. It all just hit me that this is happening. All of it. It's crazy. In the best way. Just still, crazy."

Chuckling, he offers me his arm, and we walk away from Atticus.

"I'm just going to borrow her for one second." Ryder looks back, but Atticus brushes him off.

"I'll just make a coffee," Atticus says from behind us. "Take your time."

"I've been on movie sets for a long time," Ryder starts. "My first role was in one of my pop's movies. And my second, and third... Well, you know how that goes." He motions his free arm to everything around us. "This place—a set, trailers, hair and makeup—it's all like home to me. But I'll never forget in 1994, I was nominated for my first Academy Award. Now, mind you, I had already been in this industry for over twenty years by then. There I was on stage, blubbering like an idiot because until that moment, it had always been a job. A means to pay the bills. I love my life. I'm a lucky sonuva bitch to get to do what I do. I know that. But to be celebrated? To be honored? It just *feels* different. So I understand how this can be overwhelming. If there's anything I can do to help you, all you have to do is ask."

I've spent so much time putting Ryder up on a pedestal, and I was certain there was no way he could be as wonderful as I imagined. I don't like to be proven wrong very often, but in this case, I will gladly admit to being mistaken.

"I cried when I found out you were cast as Otto's father," I tell him. "Good, happy tears. I was ecstatic when I heard about Violet, and of course, Atticus, but you're, well, you're you."

Our moment is done as soon as the collective gasps from my friends begin behind us.

"Hello, darlings," Ryder greets Campbell, Nova, and Zoe without skipping a beat. "Come in, come in. How many more are we waiting for?"

"Three." Zoe smiles at his warm welcome. "Thank you so much for inviting us. I thought Atticus was joking at first."

"Thank you for creating the comic book that gave us all a job," Ryder counters.

"Oh, that's Birdie." Nova looks over at me with pride in her eyes. "*Suffra-Jette* is Birdie's world. We're all just living in it."

Ramona, Francie, and Margot join just a few minutes later, and for the first time in her whole life, Francie is speechless.

"That's everyone." Ryder calls us all toward the tables full of food. "Let's eat."

In addition to plenty of options for me to eat, Ryder has created a spread with a little bit of everything. I fill my plate with avocado toast, a spinach and feta croissant, a strawberry and cream crepe, and a smaller bowl of fruit salad. But there are also trays of eggs benedict, candied bacon, maple sausage links, bagels, assorted muffins, and scones.

Atticus must have told Ryder we all love lemonade, because in addition to the traditional orange-juice-based mimosa, there's a pink lemonade mimosa and a Bloody Mary bar.

Conversation comes easy. Ryder takes the time to acknowledge each of us, asking us questions about our individual contributions to the comic.

"This is all so fascinating," he says, looking around the table. "I honestly had no idea how much goes into even just a single issue. And the fact that you stick together for every issue is admirable." He turns to Zoe at his right. "You're the co-owner of Coolidge Comics, right?"

"I am," she tells him. "But I'm more of a silent owner. My husband was given the business by the original store owner. Isaac oversees the storefront side of things. Nova's husband, Bishop, manages the business side of the publishing house. I wasn't quite ready to say goodbye to my pencils, so when Birdie and Nova came to me with the idea of *Suffra-Jette*, I asked if I could be on."

"I had no intention of making this a business lunch," Ryder starts, apologizing to the rest of us before continuing. "But have you ladies ever thought of making another comic together? I don't know a thing about comics, but I know people. I'm also a dad of a little girl. I would love to see more of this"—he raises his hand and makes a circular motion with his index finger—"for her. More women-driven content. More women directors. Just, more."

Just when I think I could not be more awestruck by Ryder Donegan, Jr., he goes and shows off his feminist stance.

"I have a production company," he continues. "What would you say about starting a conversation for an exclusive comic turned into a movie? We can figure out all the technicalities during an actual business meeting, but I have a feeling you ladies are just getting started, and I want to be a part of it."

"You're being serious?" I'm glad Francie has no nerves in her body and can ask the question we all want to.

"One hundred percent," Ryder assures her, and all of us, really, without even knowing it. "You don't have to say yes or no right now. I just need to know if this is a conversation we can continue on another day."

"I think I can speak on all our behalf when I say we would absolutely love to continue this conversation with you," I tell him.

Until Atticus squeezes my hand under the table, I'm fairly certain I'm either hallucinating or dreaming. All I know is that if this is a dream, I don't ever want to wake up.

ATTICUS 33.

WITH FULL BELLIES and happy hearts, we all express gratitude for an afternoon of delicious food and wonderful, easy conversation before saying goodbye to Ryder around seven o'clock. With the overflow of joy that filled the tent, I didn't realize how much time had gone by until Ramona mentioned getting home to relieve her mom from babysitting duties.

"I just have to get my house keys and my script so I can run through tomorrow's lines," I tell Birdie as we walk in the direction of my trailer.

I'm done on set for the day, but I was in such a rush to get to Birdie earlier that I left a few things behind.

On the way, Shawn—one of the set security guards—stops us. He's a general guard, but I'm sure he spends most of his time around my trailer because he's learned that Birdie brings in treats for everyone.

On the outside, he's a giant—broad shoulders and muscles bigger than my head—but on the inside, he's a softie who jams out to Taylor Swift and loves strawberry-jam-filled donuts. We've had some great talks while enjoying early morning pastries and coffee while I'm in the makeup chair.

So much so that I've considered bringing him on to my security team after the movie wraps up.

"You heading out?" I ask.

Shawn lets out a little laugh. "Nah. Just a break for food. You two have a nice night, though."

When we get to the trailer, the door is ajar. I glance around and see Shawn's replacement not too far from us. After flagging him down, I ask him about the door because Shawn never said anything to me about it.

"Oh yeah. Your assistant is in there," he starts. "She just got here a couple minutes ago."

My stomach twists. My assistant is in London on her honeymoon. Whoever's in there isn't Diane. Birdie's eyes narrow in suspicion because she knows this too. Birdie is the one that helped me pick out Diane's wedding gift last week.

"Stay here," I tell Birdie before turning to the security guard. "I need you to call Shawn, now. Tell him I need him with Birdie."

The security guard's eyes widen when he realizes what I'm not saying.

I skip every other step up to the trailer, then push the door open all the way before stepping inside. I leave the door open, not knowing what to expect or how fast I might have to make an exit.

A woman with bleach blonde hair in a *Suffra-Jette* T-shirt and a holey pair of jeans greets me with an ear-to-ear smile. Two mugs, one that held my coffee and the other that had Birdie's tea from this morning, still sit on the table in front of her.

Definitely not Diane.

I know her, though. I can't place where I've seen her, but I *have* seen her before. Her eyes are sunken with dark circles underneath. Smeared streaks of blush are strewn across her cheeks, and a deep shade of red covers her lips.

"Hi there." I wave slowly.

I can't be sure, but I assume the woman pretending to be Diane is a fan of mine. The *Suffra-Jette* shirt throws me off a bit. No matter the situation, she lied to get in here. There's no safe way to end something like this. This isn't the first time I've dealt with a fan overstepping, but I'm never quite prepared to deal with it when it's happening.

"I'm Atticus, but I think you know that." I chuckle, trying my best not to show any sign of worry. Based on appearance alone, the frail woman in front of me doesn't look like she could do much damage to another human. All it takes is pulling out a weapon, though.

This might be a superhero movie, but we're all human, and none of us can repel bullets.

"Everything okay?" Birdie's soft voice behind me sends a jolt of panic coursing through my entire body.

Where the fuck is Shawn?

"You bitch!" The blonde woman lunges, and I step forward, putting myself between Birdie and her. She barrels into me, and stumbles back for just a moment before she tries her best to reach around me to get to Birdie.

"Damn it, Birdie, *go*," I plead. "I can't deal with this if I'm worrying about you. I need you to go."

"*This?* Deal with *this*?" The woman in front of me shouts in my face. "Don't you know who I am? Don't you know how much I love you?"

Birdie

I DON'T HAVE TIME TO TELL ATTICUS THAT I'M NOT going anywhere until I know he's safe when I'm pulled back out of the trailer by my waist.

"It's just me. It's just me," Shawn assures me as he carries me down to the pavement lot the trailers sit on. Once my feet are on the ground again, he shakes his head. "Birdie, I need you to stay here. I already called the police. They'll be here any minute. Atticus is going to be okay but—"

"I've seen her before," I tell him. "She was in Lupine Cove last weekend. At the coffee shop and comic shop. She must have followed me."

My stomach tightens when I remember that I left from my house.

What if she knows where I live? What if she followed me to Zoe's?

The thought of her watching the house makes my stomach twist. I have never felt so violated. And the fact that I unknowingly put my friends in danger too? Blood-boiling rage fills me.

"No matter what you hear in there, you stay out here. Do you hear me?" Shawn asks, narrowing his eyes toward the additional security guard, who nods in understanding. Shawn's tone is assertive—nothing like how he's ever spoken to me before. "I'm going to get Atticus out of this, but I need you to just hang tight for a second, okay?"

Shawn opens the door and before sticking his head into the trailer. "I had security escort Ms. Yamamoto off the set for the time being, sir. I would feel better if—"

I can't make out anything else Shawn says as he closes the trailer door behind him.

In the minutes that follow, everything feels like a chaotic blur. Police officers arrive on scene, and a small group of people from the set have collected around Atticus's trailer—including Zoe and Nova, who had come this way to see if Atticus and I wanted to join them and their husbands for dinner tonight. One of them stands on each side of me. Nova has her arm linked loosely in mine, while Zoe has a tight grip on my hand.

It's like they know I need to be held in place, or I'm going to storm the trailer again. I have *somehow* managed to keep my composure throughout this ordeal, even when the bubbling urge to let out a piercing scream is just shy of hitting the surface.

All the while, Atticus and Shawn are still in there with a mentally unstable woman.

What if she hurt Atticus? I didn't see a weapon, but that doesn't mean she doesn't have one. Why hasn't Shawn come back out? Where was the rest of the security as she lied her way through the gates? She's clearly not Atticus's agent. What is taking the officers so long to come back out?

I suck in my breath as the trailer door opens. A police officer steps out, followed by the blonde woman and another officer behind her. Shawn comes out next, scanning the crowd. He stops looking when he finds me, Nova, and Zoe, acknowledging us with a small nod.

As officers lead the woman away, she looks forward. Stopping when she gets right in front of me, she locks eyes with me, and her lips curl into a maniacal smirk, like somehow, despite being escorted out by the police, she's still won.

Right on the heels of the last police officer, Atticus emerges from the trailer. Multiple people are calling his name, but he beelines right for me. Zoe and Nova release their holds on me just in time for me to run into his arms.

As soon as he pulls me close to him, his body relaxes slightly.

"Are you okay?" he asks, stepping back, looking me over. "I'm so sorry. I'm so fucking sor—"

Cutting him off, I pull him back to me by his waist, burying my face in his chest.

After a few minutes, Shawn clears his throat and tells us that the police need both of us to go down to the station to make a statement.

"We'll be right there," Atticus says, his arms still wrapped tightly around me.

After he wipes the tears from my cheeks, he leans in and

presses his forehead to mine. "I would have died before I let anything happen to you. I need you to know that."

Maybe it's the adrenaline still coursing through my veins, or maybe it's the reverence in his voice as he says those words to me, but I think I may have just fallen in love with Atticus Cohen.

BIRDIE 34.

I'M FAIRLY certain the officers of the Evans Police Department get people to talk based on the fear of hypothermia.

Even with the sweatshirt Atticus grabbed me from his car, I'm still shivering. The cool air from the duct above us blowing directly on me is a little unnecessary for early April in Massachusetts. That's not to say the detective and secretaries that have been assigned to the case haven't been accommodating. Someone ordered pizza at one point—I couldn't eat it because there was pepperoni on it, but the thought was nice—and I think I've drank four cups of their shitty burnt coffee. I don't drink coffee too often, but even I know this is garbage bean water.

We've been sitting here for four hours now. At this point, it's just a waiting game. During that time, we've learned that Katie Wallis, a twenty-two-year-old from Los Angeles, has been following me for about a month now.

As an aspiring actress, she was an extra on Atticus's last movie, and that's where she "fell in love." If this were a Hallmark movie, their meet-cute would have changed the future entirely.

The abridged version is that Katie was late to set, wasn't watching where she was going, and ran into Atticus. He helped her pick up all her belongings and asked her if she was okay.

Once he was sure she was fine, Atticus went about his day, and the next day, and the one after that, and never gave Katie Wallis a second thought. Katie, on the other hand, began a full-fledged obsession that led her to pack up her car and drive across the country when she found out he was dating someone else—*me*.

She was trying to catch me doing something that would make me unworthy of Atticus's love. She hadn't found anything, but she had come to the trailer tonight to try to get Atticus to see that *she* loved him. She knew I didn't love him. She knew I was a gold digger just trying to advance my own career. And if tonight didn't work, she was going to "try something else."

Apparently, she told the detective she just wanted Atticus to see how much she was willing to do to show him her love. And then came the video call from Campbell. Dozens of cars and news vans are currently parked along our street, waiting for me to come home. As it turns out, Katie Wallis also posted our address on Twitter before she ambushed the set.

She claims she doesn't know Atticus's—her intent was to either dig up enough dirt on me to bring to Atticus or scare me away. Unfortunately for her, I've been faithful to Atticus. Even when it was all fake.

"Tell Campbell to head to my house." Atticus sighs. "Neither of you is going home until we sort this out. You'll stay with me. At least then I'll know you're both safe."

"That sounds like a good idea," Detective Whitehall agrees. "I can put in a call to the Concord Police Department as well. They can survey the area before you leave here and keep your neighborhood in rotation during patrol."

Before we leave, Detective Whitehall hands us each one of his cards and goes over the terms of the emergency temporary restraining order with us.

As hard as he tries to reassure us that a piece of paper will keep her away, I know nothing will stop her if she really wants to get to us. *To me.*

"Are you hungry?" Atticus asks as we walk out of the precinct. "We can stop and get food on the way home."

"Honestly, no," I tell him. "I just want to go to bed and forget this whole night ever happened."

That won't happen for a while, though. I have a phone full of unanswered texts. At the very least, I need to call my mom and dad, who have called me from their cell phones and the landline number they keep at the house for emergency purposes. Atticus needs to call his aunt and his sister.

"I will call your parents and my aunt," he says, opening the car door. "I'll send out a group text to the *Suffra-Jette* crew to let them know we're all okay and that you and Campbell are at my house for the time being. You are going to take a bath and go to bed."

Pinching my eyebrows together, I look up at him. For the first time since we got to his trailer, his face softens.

"What?" He shrugs. "I know my girl. You're worrying about everyone else right now. I'll take care of it. All you have to do is decide how hot you want the water and if you want to use the jets in the Jacuzzi."

My girl.

He says it with such ease. Like I've been his girlfriend for more than half a day. Well, I mean, legitimately. Time has made no sense today. Our afternoon in the kitchen and lunch with Ryder and the girls felt like it went by in the blink of an eye. Hours passed by like minutes.

But from the moment Atticus stepped into that trailer alone, the clock stopped. Mere seconds had the same effect as hours of passing time. The last six hours have sucked up days' worth of energy.

"That sounds wonderful," I admit before he closes the door and walks around the front of the car to the driver's side.

We don't say anything else as he starts the ignition and pulls out of the parking lot. My eyes grow heavier with every passing mile as Sammy Rae and The Friends plays from the speakers. With his hand wrapped in mine, I know I'm safe to rest my head. And so, I succumb to my exhaustion, thankful I still have his hand to hold tonight.

ATTICUS 35.

IT'S BEEN five days with my temporary housemates.

There has been no filming since Monday. The production company sent out a mass email saying set would be shut down temporarily while new security measures are implemented. Haley reached out to both Birdie and me to tell us she would personally do anything needed for us to feel safe on set again. Violet and Ryder both sent flowers to Birdie, and Ryder had an entire catered dinner sent to my house on Tuesday night. Between that and the food from Birdie's parents and Aunt Bea, my fridge is packed.

Campbell has all but taken over my home office. Which is fine —at least someone is using it. My publicist flew in from Los Angeles, and between the two of them, Birdie and I don't have to worry about a damn thing. Well, as far as press and making statements go. Neither of us wants to do any kind of interview. We just want to move forward and forget the whole thing ever happened. Though from her new jumpy demeanor and the way she leaves a trail of lights on behind her after the sun goes down, it's safe to say it's still very much in the forefront of Birdie's thoughts.

Parker senses the shift. He follows her around everywhere. I've always joked and said he's the worst guard dog ever, but he's doing his job right now. He knows she doesn't feel safe. He knows he needs to be with her right now, and I can't fault him for that. If she wouldn't get annoyed with me, I would follow her around too.

She keeps telling me that she's fine, but I know she's not.

It's been five days since the incident, and the paparazzi and press were still waiting for us outside on their street this morning when we went to get more of their clothes.

Their landlord has called Birdie every day to relay the messages he's getting from upset neighbors. And every day, Birdie tells him that they're still not home and to call the police. Cash has been driving by to give Campbell updates, but it doesn't look like they're leaving anytime soon. The press conference Detective Whitehall gave on the "stalking incident on the *Suffra-Jette* set" this morning.

There's only one option right now, and neither Campbell nor Birdie is going to like it. Their address is out there now. Even when this slows down and becomes yesterday's news, it's not safe for them to stay there anymore. What's to stop Katie or anyone else from going there?

It's a rented condominium. I cannot upgrade the security system or put a privacy fence around their yard. I already looked into it and was shot down on both accounts by the homeowner's association of their complex.

"Do you both have a second?" I ask.

I don't know when I'll get them both in the same room again, so it's now or never. I'd love to say that having Birdie here has been a blissful staycation, but much like her best friend, she has chosen to dive deep into her work. While Campbell has my office space, Birdie has been ferociously writing in a notebook in the sunroom. On the warmer days, like today, she goes out to the patio and doesn't come back in until dinnertime.

"I have about ten minutes," Campbell answers, looking down at her phone. "I have a call with Bishop at one o'clock."

"Okay, I'll be quick," I assure her, glancing over at Birdie. She doesn't say anything, but she places her notebook on the table, giving me her undivided attention. "You can't go back home. It's not safe anymore. And as much as I love having you here, I know this isn't home either."

"Are you kicking us out, Atticus?" Campbell teases.

"No, no." I shake my head, turning to Birdie when I say, "I am not kicking you out. But I am offering to pay for all moving expenses and a year's rent. All of this is because of me—"

"None of this is because of you." Birdie speaks for the first time since we got back from their house. "We cannot ask you to do something like that, Atticus. It's too much."

"You didn't ask, though." I shrug.

Birdie's shoulders rise and fall with her breath before she turns to Campbell. "Can you give us a few minutes?"

Campbell's eyes fill with concern as she looks back and forth between the two of us. She squeezes Birdie's shoulder gently and says, "I'll just be in the office if you need me."

"Campbell and I talked to our parents," she starts. "We're going to stay with them until we find a new place. I was going to tell you tonight. My dad and Cash are going to start packing up the big stuff this weekend."

My stomach drops. "I hope I didn't say or do anything that made you feel like you aren't welcome here. There's no rush for you to leave. You can stay here as long as you want—or need to."

"It's not that," she says. "We're both so grateful for you letting us stay here, but this is *your* house."

With a single snap of a second, memories of the past come rushing back to me. As much as I don't want to acknowledge it, the parallels between now and the beginning of the end of my last meaningful relationship are undeniable. Gemma was in this industry, and she had been tormented by the press, paparazzi followed her everywhere, and when shit hit the fan, when it all became too much, she went to go stay at her mom's "for a few days."

A few days away from all the madness made her realize she couldn't do it anymore—she couldn't be with me anymore.

I can't go through this again. More importantly, I can't let Birdie go through this. Because as long as she's with me, she's not safe. Everything that happened with Katie could have been worse. She could have had a weapon at the trailer. She could have attacked Birdie at home.

I can't keep Birdie protected. The only way to ensure her well-being is to put a stop to this. All of it. I want to do anything but end this. What other choice do I have? Continue to put her in harm's way?

I don't make a habit out of living in fear, but this is controllable. This is something I can change. It will be tabloid fodder for a while, but eventually, Birdie will get her life back. Right now, according to the press, she's Birdie Yamamoto—girlfriend of Atticus Cohen. Which is bullshit anyway. But in time, she'll be known for being the writer of *Suffra-Jette* again. When that happens, she won't have assholes with cameras in her face at the grocery store or chasing her out of her home.

"I know being with me is a lot to take on, and I can't ask you to take on more. I was selfish wanting you to be mine." I swallow. "When we were just pretending, it was easier to think this wouldn't happen, but we need to talk to Campbell about making a statement. We need to end this, Birdie. Really end this."

"I'm sorry. What?" As she stands up from the table, her eyes furrow in confusion. "No. No. Absolutely not. Atticus, it was *one* day. One difficult day. We can figure this out."

Every word she says is a knife slicing through me.

The air in this house is so goddam thick... or I'm just suffocating in this moment.

I've participated in my fair share of breakups in my life. I have been heartbroken and the heartbreaker—but this time it feels like both. No matter how much it hurts me, though, saying goodbye to Birdie is for the best. Certainly not for me, but for her. And that's what matters. *She's* all that matters.

What a bullshit time to realize you're completely, irrevocably in love with someone.

I let out a breath before I reiterate my point.

I don't know what else to say. I don't want to end this. I don't want to hurt her. I don't want any of this.

"You're here in hiding, Birdie. You can't even go home. There's no figuring anything out. We need to end this so you can live your life. So you can be safe again. So your friends are safe again. This isn't fair to you or Campbell... or anyone on set... or your families."

It's selfish of me, but as the water pools in her eyes, I wish she would get mad instead. Throw something. Punch me. Scream. That's not Birdie, though. Even when she hated me, she did it in a way that it was only obvious to me. I wish we could go back. If she hated me, this wouldn't cut so deep. I can live with her hating me. I don't want to think about her leaving here sad, crying to her friends...

Fuck, I can't think about it. If I do, I'm going to take it all back.

"Is this because I've been distant since I got here?" she asks, her brows softening. The vulnerability in her voice is like a punch to the gut. "It's not you or anything that happened. I got an idea for a new comic Tuesday morning. I wanted to get a few issues mapped out for Nova to look at. I was thinking Zoe and Isaac could take it to their meeting with Ryder. I was hyperfocused. I'm sorry. I should have told you. I tend to get tunnel vision when I get a new idea."

"I'm really excited for you," I tell her honestly. The opportunity Ryder is offering her and the rest of the *Suffra-Jette* team is incredible. If what she creates is half as amazing as *Suffra-Jette*, they're sure to have another massive hit on their hands. "I'm sure it's going to be great, and I will always be in your corner, Birdie, but that doesn't change anything between us. We need to end this. For real."

With every furious shake of her head, slivers of my heart shatter like glass.

"No. You're making a mistake, Atticus. Please don't do this." Her bottom lip trembles as her voice starts to shake. When she reaches for me, I step back. I know the second I feel her touch, I'll cave. Birdie Yamamoto is my weakness. My Kryptonite. "When everything settles down, you're going to remember why you wanted to make this 'real' and I... I will be at my parents' house. I won't wait forever, but I know this isn't the end for us. I know it. It can't be."

It has to be.

BiRDiE 36.

FOR THE SECOND time since Atticus Cohen came into my life, I run from him. This time, I leave everything behind. I don't care about my clothes or my work. None of that seems important right now.

And if having my heart broken in a kitchen on a Friday afternoon wasn't hard enough, there's a sweet husky waiting for me by the front door, undoubtedly thinking we're about to go for a walk or for a ride.

Parker has been my shadow the last five days. He's waited for me outside the bathroom while I've showered. He slept right in between me and Atticus but always had a paw on me. Even if Atticus woke up before me, Parker stayed in the bed until I got up.

We ate breakfast together. I took him on his walks. The front passenger seat of my car is now covered in his fur from our daily trips to Starbucks for my Iced Chai and, of course, a Puppuccino for Parker.

Atticus made a joke a few days ago that Parker was my dog now.

He isn't, though. Which means I'm losing him too. I don't know what hurts more.

Goodness knows I didn't have "falling in love with Atticus Cohen and his perfect pup" on my bingo card.

"No, Parker. Stay." I pull in my bottom lip, biting it as hard as I can handle, willing the tears to stay in my eyes for just a few minutes more.

I didn't let Atticus see me cry. I'm determined to make it out of his house before I lose my composure. Right now, I'm teeter-tottering on an incredibly thin line. The sweet husky with his tail wagging by the door might just be what makes me crack.

Bending down, I kiss his nose and he nuzzles into my face.

"You have to stay here, bud," I whisper. My chest aches more with every word that leaves my lips. "I have to go."

Standing up, I motion for him to stay, and I open the front door just enough to squeeze out of it by myself. As soon as I pull it shut behind me, he lets out a howl. Even through the hard wooden door and the closed glass portion of the screen door, I can hear his sadness.

Animals are so much smarter than we give them credit for. Parker might not understand exactly what just happened, but he knows it's nothing good.

With shaking hands, I put the keys in my ignition and begin to back out of the long driveway that leads to Atticus's house. Until this very moment, I had been grateful for the separation it gave us from the rest of the street. Now it just seems like with every passing inch of pavement, I'm moving further away from Atticus and Parker.

I drive as far as my eyes will allow. When the lines on the road blur from the tears pooling in my eyes, I pull over on the side of the road.

As soon as I'm in the safety of the breakdown lane, I let out a guttural scream.

This is what I've been avoiding. I have kept high walls around my heart because I never wanted to feel like this. For someone who needs to be in control of everything, who needs to have a plan at all times, I don't know what I'm supposed to do. How am I supposed to keep going knowing every mile I drive I'm agreeing that it's over between us?

We barely touched the surface of what we could be. It wasn't enough. I was supposed to visit him wherever his next movie took him. His nieces are expecting us to come over for a movie night tomorrow. He needs to go to a baseball game with my dad. There's a new Spider-Man comic we have to get next month.

We can't be over. We didn't even get the chance to start.

Damn it, why did Atticus have to go and prove he isn't a piece of shit? This would be so much easier if I still hated him. If I didn't know that he doesn't want this.

If I thought for one second that he genuinely wanted to walk away, I would be able to be angry with him. I could paint him as a womanizer, accuse him of using his words to get into my pants just to walk away. Just because he knew he could. But he's doing this because he feels he has to. He thinks it's the only way to keep me safe.

Part of me wishes he had lied. If he had said it never meant anything to him, that *I* never meant anything to him, I would be halfway to my parents' already. I can't be mad at him. I can be mad at everything that led us here, but not him.

I just want to feel anything but this.

It's four o'clock. There's only one person I know I can count on to get me right now. And as much as I hate to call him, I can't sit on the side of the road miles from Atticus's house forever.

"Cash, I need you."

CAMPBELL 37.

THIS IS MY FAULT. I pushed them into their fake relationship in the first place. I'm the one that continued to plant the seed of possibility in Birdie's ear. She's always been the sensible one when it comes to love.

Well, with the exception of Cash.

Birdie is my best friend. She's the sister I never had. Which is why, as much as I love my little brother, I always hoped she would snap out of whatever spell he had her under. She's too damn good for him. She always has been.

She deserves the kind of man that shows up for all the things. She deserves a man that invites her to a gala and makes sure that not only she's taken care of but her friends are too. Not because her friends need him to send them expensive designer dresses and shoes, but because he knew it would mean a lot to her. She deserves the kind of guy that goes on strawberry picking dates with the children's home that holds such a big piece of her heart. The guy that not only supports her dreams and goals but champions them.

Cash never would have been that man, but Atticus was. Atticus is.

I cannot describe how gut-wrenching it was to see him fall to the floor as soon as the front door closed. I was supposed to be in the office, but my intuition told me to stay close by. I should have interjected, but I understand why Atticus is doing this.

Hearing that a stalker had been following Birdie and knows where we live is terrifying in itself, but then having our address leaked for the world to know... I'm glad our parents asked us to come home, because I would never feel safe at the condominium after all this. She would never tell Atticus so, but neither would Birdie.

"What can I do?" I ask Atticus.

"We need to make a statement," he starts and sighs. "I would really appreciate if you touched base with my publicist before posting anything. Make it a joint statement. I got some shit the last time."

"I'll take care of everything, but I should have phrased that better," I say. "Birdie isn't going to go home. Well, not to the condo anyway. She's safe at her parents' house. A statement can wait till tomorrow—or even Monday. Right now, I need to know what I can do as a friend for you."

"Birdie left so fast that there's no way she took any of her stuff with her." Atticus pushes himself off the floor. "Can you make sure she gets her notebook? She was working on a new comic to take to Ryder."

"I heard." I nod. "She meant what she said. When she gets a new idea, it becomes an obsession. We weren't living together yet when she first got the idea for *Suffra-Jette*. I didn't hear from her for a week. When I showed up on her doorstep, worried because she had never ghosted me before, she was in desperate need of a shower and something other than Red Bull in her system."

Before he can answer, my phone rings in my hand. My brother's name shows up on my phone and, for the first time ever, I almost send him to voicemail.

"Hey, little bro," I say, hoping my voice doesn't give me away. "What's up?"

I glance over at Atticus and point in the direction of the sunroom. I'm sure the last person Atticus wants to hear about is Cash.

"Birdie just called me," he says, his voice filled with the same worry I feel. "She asked me to go pick her up. She's sitting on the side of the road in Concord. I'm already on my way, but do you think after I get her, you could have Atticus bring you to her car and drive it back to Annie and Ken's? I can drive you back down later to get your car too. I just don't want to leave Birdie's car on the side of the road to be towed."

"Birdie called you?" I ask lowly. Of all the people to call, I didn't expect it to be Cash. I'm not sure what happened that day at family dinner, but it was no secret things weren't exactly friendly between the two of them. "Why?"

"She knew I would come."

Fair enough. Their history might be messy, and Cash may think with the head in his pants more than the one attached to his neck, but he would never leave Birdie stranded on the side of the road.

"I'll take care of it," I assure him. "I'm going to grab all of Birdie's things too. I know she'll want her notebook."

"How bad is it, Campbell?" There's a pause on the line before my brother continues. "I need to know what I'm walking into."

Tears brim my eyes when I think of the hurt in Birdie and Atticus's hearts right now. My stomach knots picturing Birdie sobbing on the side of the road as she waits for Cash. The sound of Parker's howl when Birdie walked out the door plays in my head on repeat as I try to produce an answer for Cash.

"She loves him enough to stay, and he loves her too much to let her."

ATTICUS 38.

CASH.

Of all people, she called Cash.

I don't have any right to feel angry, but that doesn't change the fact that I do. Birdie isn't vindictive. There's no way she ran right to bed with another man, but I can see him trying to "comfort" her under the guise of friendship now. He certainly wouldn't be the first asshole to take advantage of a vulnerable woman.

And there isn't a damn thing I can do about it.

I'm the one that let her go.

It's been five hours since Birdie left. Four and a half hours since I took Campbell to Birdie's car parked on the side of the road just a few miles from my house. Two hours since I found the oversized X-Men T-shirt she wore to bed last night on the floor next to her side of the bed and broke down, clutching it to my chest like it was something sacred. An hour since I lost my temper and threw an empty mug she left in the sunroom against the wall because I caught sight of the lip gloss stain on the brim.

Parker has only left his spot by the front door to eat and go to the bathroom once. Every noise outside gives him hope. So when the doorknob begins to jiggle, his ears perk up. At the sound of the front door pushing open, I brace myself.

Because there are only two other people who have keys: Aunt Bea and my sister.

"Oh, Atticus." Eliza steps into the foyer and drops her purse to the floor at the sight of me, sitting at the bottom of the stairs. Parker isn't the only one foolish enough to have false hope.

"Not that I'm not always happy to see you, sis." I muster enough strength to give her a weak attempt at a smile. "But tonight's probably not the best night to come by for a visit."

"I know." She nods. "Birdie called me. She didn't think you should be alone. I would have been here sooner, but there was a bedtime catastrophe, and then Mila needed three goodnight stories."

"You could have just called to check in, you know."

"So you could lie and tell me you're okay? I think not, little brother," Eliza says, lowering herself to the staircase. She nudges me to make room for her on the step I'm sitting on. "What happened?"

"There are eighteen other steps." I glance over my shoulder at the rest of the staircase. "Is there any reason you also need to sit on this particular one?"

"Stop deflecting," she says, taking the empty glass that once held expensive bourbon. The kind meant to be sipped and savored. Not chugged like ten-dollar gas station beer. When I don't answer her, she repeats herself. "Atticus, what happened?"

"I fell in love with her, Liza." My shoulders slump in defeat. "So the rest of the world now feels entitled to her. We went to Birdie and Campbell's condo to get some of their belongings earlier, and they chased us to the front door. We had a police escort, and that didn't matter to any of them. They just wanted to capture her because she was with me. They wanted to see her crying or scared or, God forbid, angry. Birdie Yamamoto is everything that is good in this world. She doesn't deserve this."

"But *you* didn't do this," my sister argues. "You're not the one that posted her address online. You're not the one who chased her for a photograph. If anything—"

Standing up, I shake my head. "You don't understand. It will never stop. If it's not someone like Katie Wallis, it's Jason Franco of Pow! Press trying to pit us against each other. Birdie will never be safe if she's with me."

"We take a chance every single day simply by getting out of bed," Eliza says.

"You think I didn't try to justify that myself before letting her walk out the door?" I chuckle, stopping her before she has the chance to remind me any one of us could get hit by a car crossing the street. "This is the only way. Eventually, her world will go back to normal. Once she loses the attachment to me, she will get to live her life again. Safely."

Eliza's silence speaks for itself. My sister, the one who always has a rebuttal to everything, knows I'm right.

"There has to be some other way," she says, shaking her head. "This can't be the only solution."

"Now you sound like Birdie." I crack my first genuine smile this morning. "She pretty much said the same thing."

"Because she loves you too." Eliza looks down at Parker. "And him too. When she called, she asked me to check on *both* of you. How about you spend the night at my house? I don't think being alone in this big empty house will do either of you any good."

"I'm going to assume that politely declining isn't an option."

Eliza doesn't say anything else before turning her entire body toward the front door. "Parker! Want to go for a *ride* to Auntie Liza's house?"

For the first time since Birdie walked through that door, his tail wags. When my sister reaches for the hook that holds his leash, he stands up and barks.

"Let me pack a bag." I sigh.

I would like nothing more than to drown my sorrows in bourbon until I can't feel them anymore, but taking Parker to Eliza's house might help him forget about how much he misses Birdie. For a little bit anyway.

Yeah. It's for Parker. All for Parker.

It doesn't take me long to throw a few things together. No one at my sister's house gives a shit what I look like or what I'm wearing. When I rejoin Eliza and Parker in the foyer, she already has Parker leashed and holds one of the plastic bowls that contain his food from the fridge.

"I'm going to want breakfast, too," I joke, pulling my phone out of my pocket. No missed calls. I remotely lock the front door in the app for my security system and shove my phone back into my pocket, disappointed in myself for... well, feeling disappointed Birdie didn't call.

Atticus Cohen, pity party for one.

"How about banana chocolate chip pancakes?" Eliza offers my childhood favorite while she lets Parker into the back seat of her SUV. "Come on. I'm driving."

"Has anyone ever told you you're bossy?" I tease as I walk to the other side of the car.

"Yeah, you," she says, shutting the door behind Parker and opening her own. When we're both settled into our seats, she looks over. "You good?"

"No." I shrug, answering honestly. "But I'm ready to go."

BIRDIE 39.

ON ANY GIVEN DAY, I love and appreciate the fuss my mom makes every time I walk through the door of my childhood home. I still appreciate it tonight, but I really don't need or want pepper-mint tea or shower steamers or food or a relaxing cucumber face mask.

Despite having a bedroom of my own—in the condominium I can't go back to—my parents have never turned my bedroom into an office or a home gym or even a guest room. It's still *my* room.

It's exactly as I left it before heading to Boston for college. Posters from the first two Spider-Man movies still hang on the wall. Boxes and boxes of comic books line the floor. There's a photo strip from the local theater of me and Campbell from when we were sixteen and seventeen tucked inside the vanity mirror. The nostalgia is oddly soothing.

If there are any clothes left in my dresser, I can no longer fit in those, but Campbell brought me my clothes from Atticus's—save for my favorite sleep shirt I left on his bedroom floor this morning—and my writing notebook, so I have everything I need here.

Including a brand-new television my parents came home with when they realized I would be staying here for a bit. Climbing into bed, the combination of the same laundry detergent and dryer sheets my mom has used for as long as I can remember is comforting.

There's a light rapping on the closed door, and I sigh. I love my mom, and I know she's trying so hard to make it better, because that's just what moms do, but I'm certain my dad is the only man she's ever loved. I don't think she realizes you can't fix heartbreak with warm tea or rom-coms—even *if* they do have Ryan Reynolds and Betty White in them.

"Hey, pumpkin. Can I come in?" my dad calls from the other side of the door.

It's after ten o'clock at night, which means it's already two hours past his typical bedtime. He may have retired last year, but his body hasn't gotten the memo yet. He's still awake by four o'clock every day—the same time he left for work for over twenty years.

"Sure." I pull the blankets up over my lap and point to the television across the room. "You know, you didn't have to go buy a new TV for me. I appreciate it, but I don't want you—either of you—to make a fuss out of the fact I'm here."

My dad narrows his eyes in my direction. "If you don't think your mom is going to make a fuss over you every second you are home, you've clearly underestimated Annie Yamamoto. And I have nothing to do now *but* fuss over you, so you should just accept it."

Shaking my head, I roll my eyes. "You're incorrigible. Both of you. There's no need to fuss over me. I'm—"

"Our daughter," he says gently, taking a seat on the edge of the bed. "Whether you are eight or twenty-eight or ninety-eight. It's our job to worry, fuss, and do everything in our power to make sure you're okay and taken care of. That doesn't change just because society says you're an adult."

He pauses for a moment before he asks, "Do you remember what I would say when you would challenge the rules when you were a teenager?"

"Your house, your rules," I answer without hesitation.

If I had a dollar for every time he said that growing up, I would be a millionaire... multiple times over.

"Same applies today," he says. "I know you're an incredibly strong, independent young woman, but the situation you have found yourself in—through no fault of your own, might I add—is unlike anything you've ever experienced. I also know you don't need me or your mom as much these days, but while you're here, in our house, your childhood home, I need you to promise me you're not going to shut us out, okay? Especially your mom. We'll give you whatever you need—space, love, all the time you need. Just don't shut us out."

It's like he's known me my whole life and expects me to close everyone off to try and deal with whatever I'm feeling on my own... *or something.*

Nodding in understanding, I'm surprised by the water pooling in my eyes. I didn't think I had any more tears left in me to cry.

Leaning over, he wipes the tears from my cheeks. "We'll get you through this, pumpkin. I promise."

For the first time in my life, I don't believe the words coming out of my dad's mouth. It's not because I don't have faith in my parents. There isn't a single shadow of a doubt they would move heaven and earth for me, but they're only human. Unless one of them has been holding out and they have magic powers or a potion to make me forget Atticus, Parker, and how being with them made me feel whole for the first time in my life.

Like they were the last little piece I was missing.

The piece I had been searching for my entire life.

For a long time, I thought that void might have been not

knowing anything about my biological parents, but being with Atticus showed me otherwise.

I could never tell my dad that, though. So, I tell him that I love him instead.

It's the only honest answer I can give him right now.

If this fake relationship, turned real relationship, turned my heart shattered into a thousand pieces has taught me anything, it's that a lie, no matter how small or harmless it seems, can very quickly snowball into something uncontrollable.

And I never want to lose control again.

BIRDIE 40.

"ARE you *sure* you're going to be okay with us leaving?"

The hesitation in Mom's voice as she latches her suitcase shut is sweet but unnecessary. It's been three weeks. Two days since I've cried. I wouldn't say I'm okay, but I'll survive long enough for my parents to go enjoy their vacation. Admittedly, even if I wouldn't, I would lie just to get them out the door. They've been planning their Alaskan cruise with The Porters for a year now. I won't be the reason they don't go.

"I promise," I assure her, glancing over to where Dad is patiently waiting.

"Come on, honey," he coaxes, reaching for her suitcase. "Bridget and Ron are waiting out front.

"We're only a phone call away," Mom says as she hands him the suitcase. "I can get a flight home anytime. All you have to do—"

I reach for her hand and then give it a little squeeze. "I just need one thing before you go."

She stops and tightens her hold on me. "Anything."

"I need you to promise me you're going to have fun, and you're not going to spend your whole vacation worrying about me," I start. "I'm going to be fine."

She still doesn't seem one hundred percent convinced as she waves goodbye from the back seat of the Porters' car, but as they drive away, a small sense of relief comes over me.

My parents have both been bending over backwards since I arrived without a moment's notice a few weeks ago.

Mom has become addicted to Pinterest. I'm fairly sure she's made it her goal in life to make every single vegetarian option on the internet. Last night, she made spicy black bean burgers and hand-cut sweet potato fries. My parents still eat meat most nights, but on the nights she tries something new, they both go all in.

Dad has made it his mission to make sure I have no downtime to stew in sadness. If I'm not working, he finds something for us to do. We've taken day trips up to the mountains, and we started a vegetable garden in the backyard. I honestly don't think either one of us has a clue what we're doing, but we'll find out if we're successful in a couple of months.

We've fallen into a routine together. I've started going up to Maine to work in the office space once a week. It originally started off as a way to give my parents a day to themselves, but once the team got wind of my weekly pop in, they all started showing up. Wednesdays have very quickly become my favorite and most productive day of the week.

Knowing my parents were leaving, I left earlier than normal today, and I'm anxious to get back to where I left off.

So as soon as I close the front door, I head to my bedroom to get my work. Since no one else is home, I decide to settle in the living room with my notebook full of ideas and the storyboard with each of the six issues of a new comic plotted out.

After our first lunch with Ryder, we met again at the *Suffra-Jette* office to discuss his vision: exclusive film and television rights to a six-comic miniseries—that's all he asked for. The rest is up to us. I had little to pitch at the time, just a base idea, but he loved it. We signed contracts before he left that day.

Our first big pitch meeting is tomorrow. There will always be a part of me that worries someone will hate my story. I don't think any writer in any capacity feels one hundred percent certain before sharing their work with the world, but for the first time, I'm okay with it.

The experience of writing *Suffra-Jette* was surreal. I second-guessed everything I did or didn't do. I obsessed over trying to make everyone happy while staying true to my authentic voice.

The idea for Ashe came in the funniest way. It was the day after the stalker fiasco, and I was still at Atticus's house, trying to open a jar of pickles of all things. In that moment of struggle, I wished I had superhuman strength. And then suddenly, the pickles didn't matter anymore because I knew the next story I wanted to tell.

I know the superhuman power has been done before in many, many comics. But what if she was sixteen, brilliant, and bullied for being the small, unathletic only child of two equally famous Olympians? Instead of spending time breaking swimming records like her mom or having the muscles to row like her dad, Asheton spends most of her time in the chem lab at school. Until a freak accident changes everything, of course.

The comic book formula is a universal one.

She spent her whole life feeling like she wasn't good enough. Even after she went through her hero transformation gaining her superstrength, there were still times she didn't feel deserving of this gift. Only because she had some help getting it. Her story poured out of me because Ashe *is* me.

Granted, I never did open that pickle jar, because as it turns out, I do *not* have superstrength, but all the mental blocks that stop Ashe from seeing her own full potential came from my own internal struggles. She is flawed. She is authentic. She is funny and feels empathy for all living things.

I don't know what will happen or how her story will be received. There's no way to tell if we'll be able to repeat the success of *Suffra-Jette,* but if I can inspire one person, that will be enough. If just one girl reads Ashe's story and sees herself in the character, I will have achieved exactly what I strived to do. And that will be enough for me.

Having that mindset and removing all that extra pressure has allowed me to build something I'm really fucking proud of. I wouldn't be human if the thought of pitching this miniseries to Ryder and his team didn't make me a little nervous, but I'm more excited than anything else.

The team is all on board. The way Nova's eyes lit up when she read the first draft of the first issue and Zoe's joy as she sketched out my vision for Ashe gave me so much hope. I have *so* much hope.

I needed this. Even if Ryder hates it and doesn't want to proceed with Ashe's story, I would not have gotten through this breakup without the drive to build this world. It gave me something to focus on, a reason to get out of bed every day, even on the days I just wanted to stay under the covers and cry.

I'm almost ready for tomorrow.

I just have to tighten up a few potential plot holes and work on the villain arc a bit more. Before I even have the chance to sit down with my work, the doorbell rings.

My dad had let me know they were expecting some packages, so I assume it's something being delivered. Tossing my notebook on the couch, I sprint to the front door to grab the package and stumble back when I see Cash Porter staring back at me.

He's still in his teacher attire, a navy blue Townsend Athletic Department polo shirt and a pair of black athletic shorts. Which, for some reason currently unknown to me, I used to think was sexy. Now, I just want to know what the fuck he's doing here. Especially considering he knows my parents aren't.

I will forever be thankful for the way he stopped everything he was doing to come to my aid when I needed someone after Atticus ended things, but that certainly doesn't mean I'm about to go backwards and start fucking around with Cash.

"I promise I'm just here as a friend," he says, holding out the box of wine he had tucked in his arm. "I'm on Magnolia duty this week, and I figured I would just pop over."

"Your parents could have just asked me. I would have fed her," I tell Cash. Pushing the door open behind me, I ask him if he wants to come in.

Best case scenario, we begin to forge our way back to a friendship.

Worst case scenario, I end up kicking him out.

I think I can handle both of those options at this point.

"I was about to order food," I lie as I walk to the kitchen. As I open my parents' junk drawer, I'm only slightly disappointed when I find the stack of take-out menus instead of a nostalgic snack drawer like at Atticus's house. "Actually, no. That's a lie. I wasn't. I don't know why I said that."

Cash's brows pinch in confusion at my admission.

"What are you really doing here, Cash?" I ask, closing the drawer.

"I just wanted to check in on you," he says with a small smile. "We haven't talked much since the night I came and got you."

"Well, in that case," I begin. "I'm okay-ish. I'm just taking it day by day. Minute by minute."

He lets out a sigh. "Talking from experience, if he doesn't see how amazing you are, he's an idiot."

His words are meant to be comforting, but all they do is anger me.

"Atticus thought it was the only way to keep me safe. You

don't get to come here and talk shit when you hid me like a dirty secret for a decade."

"You're right." Cash nods. "I fucked up in a lot of ways. And Atticus isn't me. I'm not good at this"—he points back and forth between the two of us—"part."

"And what exactly do you think this"—I mimic his motion of pointing between the two of us—"is?"

My copycat reaction earns me a small chuckle from Cash before he answers. "I honestly want to get back to a point where we can genuinely be friends again."

"I would love to get to that point too. I just don't know where to even start," I admit, shrugging my shoulders.

"I heard you're working on a new comic?" Cash offers with uncertainty. "Campbell said it's going to be bigger than *Suffra-Jette*."

"Actually, I could use some help with the villain arc." I laugh when he raises his eyebrows. "Whatcha think, *friend*?"

"I'm in."

ATTICUS 41.

IT'S BEEN TWO MONTHS. Well, technically nine weeks and two days since Birdie and I ended things. Or, rather, since I ended things with Birdie.

She hasn't come back to the set once. Not when I've been there anyway.

I didn't take that into consideration. She had been so excited to be a part of it all, to see the way everything came together before seeing the movie on the big screen, and I took that from her.

I hope every day will be the day Birdie decides to show up on set. I won't come on days I'm not scheduled on the call sheet because I don't want to ambush her if she *does* choose to come when I'm not here.

Nine weeks and two days later, I'm still searching for her every time Haley yells "Cut!" Her chair still sits in the same spot, in between Campbell's and Nova's, but it's been empty every time. As disappointing as it is to look over and see the canvas chair without her in it, I would be devastated if they took it away.

In all other aspects, despite the fact that I very much haven't, life has moved on. Parker started sleeping on Birdie's side of the bed again. A few weeks ago, I finally caved and let my housekeeper wash the pillowcases on that side because they no longer held the scent of Birdie's shampoo.

Campbell tells me Birdie's doing okay. Only when I ask, though.

Everyone seems to tiptoe around talking about her in front of me. Isaac and Bishop came over the night after we broke up with pizza and beer—neither one of them asked me a single thing about what happened. If I were to guess, they already knew before they walked through the door.

I've seen every single person in Birdie's circle of friends since the breakup, and no one has threatened bodily harm on me or given me so much as a dirty look. I genuinely expected to walk onto set the first day back and receive death threats—at the very least, from Francie.

For a little while, the girls kept their distance. After a few weeks, they slowly started waving hi or bye, and now it's like nothing changed. Except everything has and we're still missing the greatest person in our lives.

It's the last day of filming. Not just for me, but the movie is going to wrap at some point today. Of course, in a few months, we'll have to come back for reshoots, but until it's time for press junkets and photo shoots to promote the movie, *Suffra-Jette* is done.

The production company is hosting a big breakfast to say thank you to the cast and crew this morning. As much as I did not want to get up three hours before my call time to head to set, I dragged myself here for a cranberry muffin and a coffee before hair and makeup is expected to arrive at my trailer.

It's early still, so there aren't too many people here. Violet is half-ready, drinking a tea and talking to Haley. None of the *Suffra-Jette* team is here yet. Ryder hasn't arrived.

The sun hasn't risen yet, so it's no surprise that everyone is half-asleep—me included. So, when my phone vibrates in the pocket of my hooded sweatshirt, it startles me. The only live alerts I have on my phone are texting and phone calls. Everything else is silenced because if my notifications were on, my phone wouldn't stop all day.

Who the hell is texting me at five in the morning?

Campbell Porter.

"Convinced Birdie to come to set today. Picking her up in an hour. Thought you might want the heads-up."

With one single text, my heart begins to slam against my chest. In a matter of moments, I question whether it's physically possible for the beating organ to burst out of my rib cage.

As terrifying as it is, it's a nice reminder that I still have it within my body, because for a while, I was almost certain Birdie took it with her when she walked out of my house.

And, yes, I'm aware the heart isn't what dictates love. However, the way it's reacting to knowing Birdie is on her way could provide a strong counterargument.

"Atticus, you alright?" Shawn approaches me with concern in his eyes. Over the last couple of months, he and I have gotten close. So much so that I asked him to join my personal security team once the movie is done. It's hard to find people you can trust in this industry. After everything that's happened on this set, after the way he came through for me and for Birdie, I know I can trust him. "I say this with a lotta love, but you don't look so good, man."

I put down the cup of coffee on the table next to me, then wipe my clammy hand on my sweatpants. It would be safe to assume the warm beverage that had just been in my hand is responsible for the little beads of sweat in the palm of my hand, however, that leaves the other clammy hand unexplained.

"Birdie is coming to set." I lean in, lowering my voice so only he can hear. "Birdie is coming to set today, and I'm kind of freaking the fuck out."

"Because you still love her." It's not a question, so I don't bother confirming.

But, I mean, of course I still love her. I never stopped. I didn't end things with her because I didn't love her. If anything, it was because I love her too much.

That hasn't changed. In the last couple of months, I've gone through my own version of the five stages of grief. Except, instead of accepting moving on from Birdie, I've accepted that I'm just going to die alone. At first, the thought was terrifying.

As I grew into this career of mine, I imagined I was working for something more. The early mornings, late nights, traveling, sacrificing time, and missing important days with my family... It has to be for something more than myself.

Acting is important, but I've come to learn it's just a job when you don't have someone to share it with. I still give one hundred percent of myself to the character—I owe Birdie that much—but, as pathetic as it is, I just don't have the drive I did before and during my time with Birdie.

Birdie was the love of my life. She *is* the love of my life. No one could ever compete with her or with what I feel for her. Living as a perpetual bachelor holds no appeal for me. I don't want to fuck a new girl every night, and I refuse to settle with someone else.

I've put her on a pedestal. Everyone will tell you there's no such thing as a perfect person, but Birdie was *my* person.

It's cliché as fuck, I'm aware.

Now that I'm in my acceptance stage, I've learned to live with loving her, despite it all. During my denial phase, I tried to convince myself there was no way I could have loved her in such a short amount of time—that we barely knew each other. I thought if I kept feeding myself lies, I'd eventually believe them. All it did was make me realize the truth, though.

"I need to go to hair and makeup," I finally say, letting out a breath.

"No, you don't. Not yet anyway," Shawn counters. "What you *need* is to come up with a plan."

"A plan?" I repeat. "For what? I doubt she's even going to talk to me, Shawn. We threw down hard when we ended things."

"To get her back, obviously." He motions for me to follow him to an empty part of the set. "Come on. Let's figure this shit out before she gets here."

That stops me dead in my tracks. "No. It... We... I can't. You don't think I've played out every scenario that would allow us to be together? It's impossible."

"It's only impossible because you're making it that way." Shawn shakes his head. "Think objectively here for a second. She doesn't live where it's unsafe anymore. The press has moved on. So now we put in the security measures before things can get out of hand again."

The tiniest sliver of hope returns to my body for the first time since Birdie walked out my front door.

"We?" I repeat his words for the second time in a matter of minutes. "I didn't know this was a 'we' thing."

"Act like you're not going to make me her bodyguard." Shawn grins. "Birdie already knows me, and *you* know I would never let anything happen to her."

"I don't know, man," I tell him. "What if I fucked things up too much?"

"Oh, shut up." He laughs. "You're *Atticus Cohen*."

"I really hurt her, Shawn." I let out a breath. "I didn't know what else to do. I just wanted to keep her safe."

"You don't have to tell me that." He looks over, pointing to the studio door opening. "But you should tell her."

BiRDiE 42.

THIS DAY HAS BEEN PLANNED for weeks. It's taken many pep talks—both from myself and from my parents and friends—for me to be here. I even tried to cancel last night, but Campbell would *not* entertain that idea.

When I sent her a text to tell her I wasn't going, she came back with a text of her own forty-five seconds later, letting me know she would be at my parents' house to pick me up at six. I forgot to fill my dad in on the new plan of me not going to set, so he let her in the house. He even made us to-go mugs of coffee.

Mom got up just in time to send us off with the homemade granola bars she prepared yesterday, knowing damn well I would be a frantic mess today and wouldn't take time to eat. Of course she was right.

After Atticus broke up with me, I chose not to come back to set. Campbell never released a statement saying we broke up, so no one besides our friends and family knew for certain. My absence from set spoke for itself, though.

I didn't want to shift the attention from the movie production.

Atticus didn't need the distraction of me being on set. The crew didn't need the tension of us both being here. I hated missing everything, but it was more important to me for the filming go on without any added drama. Especially after the stalker incident. Besides, between Zoe and Campbell, I was kept in the loop anyway.

In the last two months, while I *haven't* been on set, I've worked on four new issues of *Suffra-Jette* and the new miniseries.

Getting dumped sucked, there's no doubt about that, but it gave my creativity a boost.

Nevertheless: I do not recommend the heartbreak method. Zero stars.

Standing outside of Studio C, I let out a breath. Campbell doesn't say anything, but she rubs my arm in reassurance. As the door opens, my stomach tightens. Every single inch of my body feels like it's on fire.

I'm here to visit everyone, but there's only one person that matters.

On instinct, on a set full of people, my eyes find him first.

His gray cotton T-shirt and blue chino pants aren't anything out of the ordinary, but man, do they look good on him. The time apart hasn't made me forget how handsome he is. However, I must have misplaced the memory of just *how* breathtakingly beautiful he is.

As soon as he walks toward us, I realize that as hard as I tried to prepare myself for this moment, I wasn't ready. Not even a little. Despite playing out every situation in my head a million times, my heart sits in my throat, the pulsating beat leaving me breathless.

I learned my lesson from the table read outfit drama, so yesterday, Campbell and I went shopping. I tried on more outfits than I care to admit, but I don't think it would have mattered if I showed up in the black wide-leg jumpsuit I'm wearing or a ratty old potato sack—I would have been just as self-conscious as he approaches me.

Do I look okay? Was this the right outfit? Is my hair alright? I should have put it up. Did I put on too much makeup? Not enough makeup? Damn, he really is good-looking.

"Hi, Birdie."

The two canvas bags in my hand fall to the ground as soon as he says my name. The heat of utter embarrassment flushes over me as I bend down to get the contents that spilled from the bag. Before I can say anything, Atticus is at my feet, scooping up the special edition comic created for the cast and crew.

Instead of our typical Jette, Zoe sketched a character that looked exactly like Violet in Jette's black suit. She's sitting on top of an electric pole with controlled sparks in her hand, just like Violet will appear to do at the very end of the movie. Granted, there's a lot of CGI and movie-making magic that allows that to happen, but I couldn't think of a more perfect scene for the cast and crew.

"What's this?" he asks, holding one up.

"We made a special edition comic for the cast and crew," I tell him. "It's the whole reason why I came today."

"Oh." His voice is laced with disappointment as we grab the last of the comics. "I mean, these are amazing. Were they your idea?"

"I'm sorry, Atticus," I say, water pooling in my eyes. "I can't do this. I thought I could, but it's too hard. I can't pretend everything is fine and that we're okay. I'm so sorry."

"Birdie, wait. Please." His words are desperate as I turn my back to leave. It's complete cowardice on my part. I've never been the girl to run from anything or anyone. Well, until Atticus. "Don't leave. It's the last day. You deserve to be here. And I need to talk to you."

Everyone on set is trying not to make it blatantly obvious they're watching us, but when I look up, far too many people begin to make themselves look busy. Everyone except our group of friends. They're all watching us.

"We probably owe it to them to stay and talk," I start, nodding in their direction. "This is the first time Bishop has made it to set, and I don't think that was coincidental."

"Do you think this is a setup?" he asks, giving everyone a little wave.

"Oh, one hundred percent," I tell him. Maybe if I pretend I'm not completely falling apart inside, it might be believable on the outside. Raising the canvas bags, I let him know I'm just going to give them to Campbell and then we can talk.

I didn't intend on having a heart-to-heart with him today, but this will be good. I can get the closure I so desperately need, because if I'm being honest with myself, I'm not over him. There isn't a single part of me that doesn't still love him. Sure, it doesn't hurt as much as it did when he told me we were over, but there's still a big piece of me—all of me—that wishes we were still together.

Handing off the bags to Campbell, I give all my friends a once-over, rolling my eyes in the midst of it. "None of you are good at hiding the fact you're staring at us."

"Who said we were trying to hide?" Francie shrugs. "I'm not hiding."

I turn back around and stop when Bishop calls out my name. "Go easy on him, okay?"

I'm so glad Isaac and Bishop have a friendship with him, but need I remind Bishop that Atticus is the one that broke up with me?

"Are you okay with going to my trailer?" Atticus asks when I return to the same spot I left him standing in. He opens the studio door and steps back, holding it open for me. "I would completely understand if you're not. We can find somewhere else, but I just figure it's close and—"

"Your trailer is fine," I assure him.

The idea sends a ripple of panic through me, but not for the reason Atticus is thinking.

The thought of being in a small, enclosed space with nowhere to hide my emotions is what worries me. For a long time, I've always been the woman who leaves before she's hurt. Even with Cash, I kept it physical and on my terms. I stopped on my terms too. I have no control over my emotions with Atticus. I can't push them away. I can't pretend they don't exist. Believe me, I've tried.

When we're in the room, Atticus closes the door behind him, making the already small room suddenly feel smaller.

"Can I get you something to drink?" he offers. "I still have your tea."

"Tea would be great," I tell him.

The next few minutes are filled with an awkward silence. Atticus at least has the excuse he's making me tea, but I just stand frozen in place.

We both know someone is going to have to break the ice and start the conversation we're here to have. I can't speak for Atticus, but I'm terrified.

What if he tells me he's been with someone else? That he's ready to move on. What if I'm the only one still stuck in this love I have for him?

"Tell me something I should know," he says softly, placing the mug of Lady Grey tea on the table next to me.

His words are reminiscent of our first date at the aquarium. And the day in his trailer when he stripped down and showed his authentic self. And the first night we were intimate together.

I miss you. I love you. I'm sorry.

When I don't answer aloud, Atticus's face softens as if he understands my unspoken truths. "Okay, I'll go first. I miss you. Parker misses you too. I was going to return that X-Man shirt you left at my house, but he sleeps with it every night. It's like his security blanket. I tried to take it once, and he growled at me."

Oh, okay. Cool. We're going right for the gut punch.

Fine, two can play that game, Atticus.

"I miss you too. And Parker. Mostly Parker, but you too," I say. I'm about to tell him that I've been getting two copies of the new *Spider-Man* every month because we were supposed to get them together, and I knew he wouldn't have time to make it to a comic shop on Wednesdays. I planned to send them to him in the mail, but I brought them with me today. My dad's ringtone plays from the pocket of my jumpsuit, and I curse as I silence it. "Shit, shit, shit."

"Did you tell him?" Atticus asks, looking down at my phone. I can't believe he remembers my dad's ringtone. "How much does he hate me?"

"I told him everything, and my mom too." I swallow. "He doesn't hate you. He just—never mind. It's not important."

"Of course it's important," he counters, his eyes locking with mine. "He just what? Finish it."

"He didn't believe it was all pretend. I tried to tell him it was, but he said that a man doesn't look at a woman the way you look at me without having real feelings involved."

I choose to omit the fact that my dad said, "A man doesn't look at a woman the way Atticus looks at you without being in love." This conversation is hard enough without throwing words like *love* into the mix.

"Then when I told them it did become real and why you ended it, they understood you were only trying to keep me safe. Fairly sure Dad used the word 'selfless,' actually."

"Real feelings?" Atticus repeats with a grin. "Birdie, I loved you. *I love you.* And I know this is a real shit time to tell you, but I do."

For months, I wished I could hear those words. I played out what I would do if he came back to me. In every situation, I told him that I loved him too, because I do. But I wasn't expecting the way they sliced through me instead.

"You can't." I shake my head. "You can't say that to me, Atticus. Not now. Not when—"

He steps forward, taking my hand in his. "I need to say something, okay? I need to just get it out, or I'm going to regret it for the rest of my life. I promise when I'm done, you can say whatever you want. You can tell me you hate me and never want to see me again, and I'll respect that. But before you do, I just need to say this."

Words fail me, so I just nod. I'm overcome with more emotions than I'm equipped to handle right now.

Fear, anxiety, and the most dangerous of all: hope.

"I can't take back what I did," he begins. "I can't and I don't think I would if I could. You are the most important person to me, and I was doing what I thought was the only thing to keep you safe. What I didn't realize is that by doing so, I would be robbing myself from feeling happy for the rest of my life. I'm talking truly, down to the core, happiness. I know I hurt you, but please believe me when I say I hurt myself too."

"Atticus," I breathe out.

It's a warning. He doesn't know it yet, but if he keeps going, I'm going to break. I'm weak. He makes me weak.

"I'm so sorry." He leans in until his forehead is touching mine, and I begin to tremble. "I'm so fucking sorry."

Swallowing, I pull myself back enough to gain what little composure I'm clinging to.

"You don't need to apologize," I tell him. "I understand you did it from a place of fear, a place of love. And, for what it's worth, I loved you too. I *love* you too."

"Tell me it's not too late," he pleads. "Tell me I can fix this. I'll do anything. Everything."

"There's nothing to fix." I shrug. At that, his shoulders slump.

"Okay." He sighs. "I understand."

"There's nothing to fix because I've always been yours, Atticus," I tell him. "I'm still yours. I left my heart with you that day. You still have it."

"There's going to be a lot to figure out," he says. "I'm going to be overprotective and worried, and you're probably going to get annoyed, but I asked Shawn to be your personal security guard."

I'm sure there's a story to that, but right now, all I want is to kiss his stupid, stubborn face.

"I kind of expected something like that, and we can go over all that later," I tell him. "But right now, I need to know this is real life. Right now, I need you to kiss me so I know this isn't a dream."

A hint of the peppermint toothpaste he uses still lingers on his tongue as he obliges my request. His kiss starts off slow, deliberate. As if he's savoring every second. God knows I am.

"I love you, Birdie," he whispers. "And I'm going to spend the rest of my life showing you just how much."

I write comic books for a living. I dance on the line of fiction and reality every single day, and I couldn't have imagined our story.

I don't know what will happen in the next chapter, but if we're in it together, I know this one ends with a happily ever after.

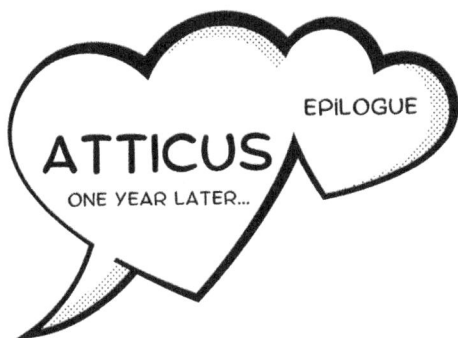

"Wow."

One word, one tiny syllable, is all I manage to get out when I see Birdie in her dress for the premiere. The custom Millie Bradley off-the-shoulder satin gown is all black except for the purple lightning bolt on the torso. The bodice tapers at the waist, transforming into a dramatic ball gown skirt that floats with every step she takes.

Her hair is out of the "deadline messy bun" for the first time in weeks, sitting in voluminous curls that fall just below her shoulders. When she gets closer, the first things I notice are the bright pop of purple eyeshadow and the dramatic black eyeliner. *That's a lie.* The first thing I noticed was how incredible her cleavage looked—the way the fabric dipped just low enough to tease without plunging down.

Nevertheless, she looks like a princess—a badass princess.

"Wow yourself. Hollywood."

As soon as they announced the date of the world premiere, we got to work on our outfits. Millie was overjoyed to get a phone call from Birdie. The two of them spent hours planning and have become friends in the process. So much so that Millie insisted the only payment she needed was for the fabric of the dress and to hook her up with a ticket to the premiere.

"You look amazing," I tell her, bending down for a kiss.

Despite being begged by the stylist to wear heels, Birdie insisted on wearing black high-top Converse. I don't blame her for wanting to be comfortable. Especially considering the plum purple suit I'm in is so far out of my comfort zone that I can't even see it anymore.

It's not necessarily the suit itself. The color certainly isn't my go-to, but it's the boldness of the black button-down with small purple lightning bolts that are hand embroidered into the fabric that has me questioning my attire.

A small knock on the hotel suite door doesn't allow me any more time to ponder over my fashion choices.

"Alright, you crazy kids." Shawn's voice booms from behind the closed door. "Time to go."

As Birdie reaches for her little purse, I stop her.

"Wait. Before we go," I begin. "I have something for you."

I go my suitcase, reaching down to the bottom and take out the box I'd hidden before we left home.

"What's this?" Her brows raise slightly as she takes the gift into her hands.

"Just a little something to celebrate tonight," I tell her as she places it down on the bed and opens it.

I knew Birdie wouldn't be impressed with jewelry. A year's worth of collecting first editions, variant covers, and signed copies of her favorite comics, however? That's something fitting for her. With a lot of help from Isaac, Bishop, and Beckett, I put together quite a collection.

The idea of proposing to her tonight had come to mind more than once. I've had Ken and Annie's blessing since I took them to lunch three months ago when Birdie was in Maine for a girls' weekend with Zoe and Gwen. Shortly after, I picked out the amethyst ring I've been carrying around with me. But I know she would be disappointed if the attention shifted from the movie to our engagement. Even if we didn't say anything, all it would take is the sight of the purple gemstone on her hand for questions to arise.

Tonight will be about *Suffra-Jette*. Tomorrow, when all the movie craziness is done and we're back home, I'll ask her to marry me. Though, at this point, I'm not sure I'll ever top the pure surprise and joy on her face as she sifts through the comics.

"What did I do to deserve you?" she asks, placing a first edition issue of the 1980 *The Savage She-Hulk* back into the box.

"I ask myself that all the time," I tell her, offering her my hand. "Come on. Let's see your movie."

Birdie

THERE'S A *PURPLE* CARPET OUTSIDE OF THE LOS ANGELES Convention Center for the world premiere of *Suffra-Jette*.

The moment we step out of the car, people are shouting for us. Atticus slides his hand in mine, using his free hand to give a general wave. He's so good at this. You would never know that these events terrify him. The anxiety of saying the wrong thing or spoiling something in the movie and talking to strangers who are just baiting me for the next headline is certainly not his favorite part about his job.

It's not something I think I'll ever get used to.

Though, I'd say I'm equal parts nervous and excited.

I cried when I saw the movie's teaser trailer. And then again when the full trailer was released at Comic-Con. I missed so much of filming when Atticus and I weren't together, and the green screen backdrop still leaves so much to the imagination. I know I'm going to be a mess from the opening scene to the end credits, and I can't wait.

As we begin to make our way to the press to take photos, I smile at the sight of Ryan Reynolds and Blake Lively walking ahead of us.

Turns out, I *did* have the power to invite Deadpool.

The next hour is a blur of hellos, hugs, answering questions from the press, and taking selfies in the fan section. By the time we take our seats, I'm ready for the champagne that is offered to us.

We were given seats in the front row with Violet, Ryder, Haley, and the producers of the film, but just before the lights dim, we head back with the rest of the *Suffra-Jette* team and our families.

Atticus and I hold hands as the movie begins to play. Seeing Violet on the screen in the set apartment brings me back to the table read for a second. So much has happened since then.

From my fake to real to broken to real again relationship. I started spending most nights at Atticus's, and eventually, I just stayed. In the last year, I've gone from Atticus's comic-book-writer girlfriend to being called Parker's mom in magazine articles. I was invited to take part in the press tour with Atticus before the movie released. After surviving multiple days of press junkets with three in the morning wakeup times, I figure we can make it through anything together.

Sometimes it still doesn't feel real. Atticus. Our relationship. This life. But I've stopped questioning it. I've stopped waiting for the other shoe to drop. I know I deserve it: the happiness, the career, Atticus's love.

Experiencing this with Atticus, my parents, and my closest friends would be more than enough, but my heart swells with joy each time the audience reacts. There's laughter, gasps, and cheers throughout. It's everything I could have ever hoped for and then some.

I manage to hold back any tears until "This Is War" by Thirty Seconds to Mars begins to play, and goose bumps trail up my arm knowing Jette's final battle scene is coming.

Lightning hits the ground on the screen, and I swear, I can feel the vibration of the earth cracking in my stomach. And even knowing that it's coming, I hold my breath when Ryder falls to the ground and Atticus holds him in his arms until Ryder's character takes his last breath. It's a testament to all their acting skills that I manage to momentarily forget that Atticus is sitting next to me—and both Ryder and Violet are just a few rows ahead of us watching the movie too.

As the movie ends, I expect us all to make our way out of the theater to head to the after-party, but I'm overcome with emotion when the entire theater erupts in applause and a standing ovation.

"You did this." Atticus leans in, whispering just loud enough for me to hear. It's the same thing he said at the table read. "All of this is because of you."

I could argue the fact there's a whole team of people that come together to make the *Suffra-Jette* comics what they are. Haley and the actors are the ones that brought the movie to life. There was a whole production crew. I'm just an exceedingly small piece of the puzzle, but he's right. I was the first piece, and Jette will always be my baby.

I just can't wait to see what happens next.

ENJOYED

THE COMIC CON...?

GO BACK TO THE BEGINNING WITH ZOE
& ISAAC'S STORY.
THE ART OF US IS COMING AUGUST
2023:
WWW.AMZN.COM/ BO9W432Q4J

ACKNOWLEDGMENTS

THE COMIC CON IS MY STORY, BUT EVERYONE KNOWS IT TAKES A VILLAGE.
AS ALWAYS, FIRST UP IS JEFFREY AND THE MINIS... JEFF. YOUR NEVER-ENDING FAITH IN ME IS WHAT GOT ME THROUGH THIS BOOK, FOR SURE. THANK YOU FOR NOT LETTING ME GIVE UP. THANK YOU FOR ORDERING TAKEOUT ON THE NIGHTS I FORGOT TO PLAN SOMETHING FOR DINNER BECAUSE I WAS SO INVESTED IN THIS STORY. FOR GIVING UP WEEKENDS SO I COULD GET AHEAD ON MY WORD COUNT. FOR GRABBING COFFEE AT 7AM AND 7PM – DEPENDING ON THE DAY. THIS MAY BE MY CAREER, BUT EVERYTHING YOU DO FOR ME AND OUR FAMILY IS WHAT MAKES IT POSSIBLE. I LOVE YOU ENDLESSLY, CRACKER JACK.
THE MINIS – DILLON, KALLIE, AND HUNTER. I AM THE LUCKIEST PERSON ON THIS EARTH BECAUSE I GET TO BE YOUR MOM. THANK YOU FOR YOUR PATIENCE AS I WROTE THIS STORY, FOR NOT COMPLAINING TOO MUCH WHEN WE HAD PIZZA TOO MANY TIMES AS I WAS GETTING CLOSE TO DEADLINE, AND FOR ALWAYS BEING SO, SO EXCITED WHEN I WRITE THE END. I LOVE YOU THREE MORE THAN ANYTHING IN THIS WORLD – EVEN MORE THAN CAPTAIN AMERICA.

MY BIG, BLENDED AMAZING FAMILY. THROUGH BLOOD, MARRIAGE, AND BY CHOICE. I AM ETERNALLY GRATEFUL TO HAVE SO MUCH LOVE IN MY LIFE. IT ALWAYS COMES IN ABUNDANCE FROM ALL SIDES, AND I KNOW JUST HOW LUCKY I AM TO HAVE THAT... TO HAVE YOU. THANK YOU FOR ALWAYS SUPPORTING THIS DREAM OF MINE.

ABBI SULLIVAN. FOR BASICALLY BEING THE BEST FRIEND A GIRL COULD ASK FOR. THANK YOU FOR ALWAYS BEING THERE TO CELEBRATE THE TRIUMPHS AND WILLING TO HOLD MY HAND DURING THE TOUGHER TIMES TOO. THANK YOU FOR ALWAYS LETTING ME BOUNCE IDEAS OFF OF YOU AND FOR KEEPING ALLLL THE SECRETS — BOOKISH OR OTHERWISE. YOU ARE THE HARRY TO MY RON, AND I HONESTLY HAVE NO IDEA WHAT I DID TO DESERVE YOUR FRIENDSHIP, BUT GRATEFUL DOESN'T EVEN COME CLOSE.

VICTORIA ELLIS OF CRUEL INK EDITING + DESIGN. BEFORE I EVEN TALK ABOUT ALL THE THINGS YOU DID FOR THIS BOOK, LET'S JUST TALK ABOUT OUR FRIENDSHIP FOR A SEC, OKAY?! YOU ARE MY SOUL SISTER. I'M NOT QUITE SURE HOW I FUNCTIONED BEFORE OUR DAILY TALKS, BUT YOU'RE STUCK WITH ME NOW. (I'D SAY SORRY, BUT I'M NOT.) THANK YOU FOR YOUR BELIEF IN THIS STORY... AND IN ME. AND, ALSO FOR EVERYTHING YOU DID FOR BIRDIE AND ATTICUS'S STORY. FROM EDITING TO FORMATTING AND BEING THE BEST DAMN HYPE-WOMAN IN THE HISTORY OF EVER. I LOVE YOUR FACE. A LOT.

AMANDA CUFF OF WORD OF ADVICE EDITING. WE GOT HERE! FINALLY! I KNOW I PROBABLY SOUND LIKE A BROKEN RECORD AT THIS POINT, BUT I APPRECIATE YOU MORE THAN YOU KNOW. THANK YOU FOR GOING THE EXTRA MILE AND LOVING ON BIRDIE AND ATTICUS THE WAY YOU DID. I WILL FOREVER BE GRATEFUL.

J.R. ROGUE. THANK YOU FOR WRITING THE MOST PERFECT POEM FOR BIRDIE AND ATTICUS. YOUR WORDS CAPTURE THEM IN A WAY THAT I DON'T THINK I EVER COULD.

JESSICA FLORENCE. I AM IN SUCH AWE OF YOU AND YOUR TALENT. THANK YOU FOR BRINGING MY VISION OF JETTE TO LIFE IN THE ART YOU CREATED.

SUZY OF CREATIONS BY SUZY. OUR COLLABS ARE MY FAVORITE BUT OUR FRIENDSHIP MEANS EVEN MORE TO ME. THANK YOU FOR ALWAYS UNDERSTANDING WHEN I GO MIA AND FOR BEING IN MY CORNER. I'M OBSESSED WITH THE SUFFRA-JETTE SCRUNCHIES... AND YOU!

SHAUNA CASEY OF WILDFIRE MARKETING SOLUTIONS. YOU WENT ABOVE AND BEYOND THIS TIME, MY FRIEND. THANK YOU FOR CHAMPIONING THE COMIC CON. THANK YOU FOR TAKING THE TIME TO READ IT EARLY KNOWING HOW MUCH THIS STORY MEANS TO ME. THANK YOU FOR EVERYTHING YOU DID LEADING UP TO RELEASE FROM COVER REVEAL TO RELEASE DAY. JUST, THANK YOU.

MY ALPHA/BETA TEAM – JULIE MOSS, DANIELE DERENZI, HALEY DAUEL, ASHLYN POWELL, TRICIA CIAK, AUTUMN WROUGHT, VIRGINIA CAREY, AMANDA MODSCHIEDLER. THANK YOU SO MUCH FOR HELPING ME SHAPE TCC INTO THE STORY IT BECAME. I AM ETERNALLY GRATEFUL FOR YOUR SELFLESSNESS WHEN IT COMES TO YOUR TIME AND YOUR FEEDBACK. I APPRECIATE YOU ALL MORE THAN WORDS COULD EVER CONVEY.

I NEED TO ESPECIALLY ACKNOWLEDGE CYNTHIA A. RODRIGUEZ AND CHRISTINA HART FOR GOING ABOVE AND BEYOND AND NOT ONLY BETA READING, BUT FOR LETTING ME TALK THROUGH ALL THE THINGS, BRAINSTORMING WITH ME, AND OVERALL, HELPING ME MAKE BIRDIE AND ATTICUS'S LOVE STORY THE BEST POSSIBLE VERSION IT COULD BE.

MY AGENT SAVANNAH GREENWELL OF TWO DAISY MEDIA. THANK YOU FOR ALL OF THE OPPORTUNITIES YOU'VE CREATED FOR ME. I CONSIDER MYSELF INCREDIBLY LUCKY TO BE A PART OF THE TWO DAISY FAMILY.

THANK YOU TO ALL OF THE AUTHORS WHO SHARED THE COVER REVEAL, READ ARCS, GAVE BLURBS, AND SHARED TCC'S RELEASE. I LOVE THIS COMMUNITY AND I CONSIDER MYSELF INCREDIBLY LUCKY TO HAVE SO MANY AMAZING PEOPLE IN MY CORNER.

ALL OF BLOGGERS, INFLUENCERS, AND READERS
WHO SHARED POSTS, CREATED EDITS, AND READ +
REVIEWED EARLY COPIES OF THE COMIC CON.
WHETHER YOU SIGNED UP VIA WILDFIRE OR YOU
WERE ON THE TCC ARC TEAM - THANK YOU FOR
TAKING TIME OUT OF YOUR LIVES TO READ AND
PROMOTE MY LITTLE BOOK BABY.
DEE'S BEES AND THE DEE HIVE - MY TWO FAVORITE
GROUPS ON THE INTERWEBS. THANK YOU FOR
CREATING NOT JUST ONE, BUT TWO, SPACES FOR
ME TO SHARE MY IDEAS, FOR FUELING MY
INFATUATION WITH CHRIS EVANS AND FOR ALWAYS
BEING SUPPORTIVE OF ME AND MY DREAMS.
THANK YOU TO THE SAN DIEGO COMIC-CON FOR
GRANTING ME PERMISSION TO USE "COMIC CON" IN
THE TITLE. I COULDN'T IMAGINE THIS BOOK BEING
CALLED ANYTHING ELSE!
SHOUTOUT TO CHRIS EVANS - WHO WILL NEVER
READ OR SEE THIS. THANK YOU FOR BEING THE KIND
OF HOLLYWOOD HOTTIE THAN INSPIRES ROMANCE
NOVELS LIKE THIS ONE. AND BIG UPS TO YOUR
PARENTS FOR CREATING SUCH A BEAUTIFUL
HUMAN.
AND, YOU. THANK YOU FOR READING THE COMIC
CON. THANK YOU FOR TAKING A CHANCE ON BIRDIE
AND ATTICUS... AND ON ME. PEOPLE LIKE YOU MAKE
MY WORLD GO ROUND. WELCOME TO THE SUFFRA-
JETTE SISTERHOOD. WE'RE JUST GETTING STARTED,
BABES. <3

ABOUT

BOOM!

DEE LAGASSE

DEE LAGASSE IS A MOM OF THREE FROM NEW ENGLAND. WHEN SHE ISN'T WRITING, SHE CAN BE FOUND HIKING IN THE WOODS WITH HER FAMILY, READING COMICS, OR HARASSING HER HUSBAND TO REACH FOR SOMETHING ON THE TOP SHELF.

EMAIL: DEE@DEELAGASSE.COM
WEBSITE: WWW.DEELAGASSE.COM
INSTAGRAM: WWW.INSTAGRAM.COM/DEELAGASSE
FACEBOOK: WWW.FACEBOOK.COM/DEELAGASSE
READER GROUP: HTTP://BIT.LY/DEESBEES
GOODREADS: HTTP://BIT.LY/DEELAGASSEGOODREADS
BOOKBUB: HTTP://BIT.LY/DEELAGASSEBOOKBUB

OTHER BOOKS

BY DEE LAGASSE

BOOM!

CAPPARELLI & CO.

WITHOUT WARNING
WWW.AMZN.COM/BO7GH7BZM2

AS FATE WOULD HAVE IT
WWW.AMZN.COM/BO7TJJR3LJ

KISMET

KISMET: A ROYAL ROMANCE
WWW.AMZN.COM/BO7M9Z961K

KISMET EVER AFTER: A ROYAL SHORT STORY
WWW.AMZN.COM/BO8P5G3ZWC

STANDALONES

MEET ME HALFWAY
WWW.AMZN.COM/BO82P8XTX1

KEEPING SCORE
WWW.AMZN.COM/BO8HM9YG5K

CONFLICT OF INTEREST
WWW.AMZN.COM/BO8XM793G1

Made in the USA
Middletown, DE
02 July 2022

68285101R00136